I0526202

Bound

The Hunter Series
Book Two

Ali Spooner

Bound

The Hunter Series
Book Two

Ali Spooner

Affinity
eBook Press
NZ
2016

Bound

© Ali Spooner 2016

Affinity E-Book Press NZ LTD
Canterbury, New Zealand

1st Edition

ISBN: 978-0-908351-73-2

All rights reserved.

No part of this book may be reproduced in any form without the express permission of the author and publisher. Please note that piracy of copyrighted materials violate the author's rights and is Illegal.

This is a work of fiction. Names, character, places, and incidents are the product of the author's imagination or are used fictitiously and any resemblance to actual persons living or dead, businesses, companies, events, or locales is entirely coincidental

Editor: Angela Koenig
Proof Editor: Alexis Smith
Cover Design: Irish Dragon Designs

Acknowledgments

I would like to thank my fans for following my stories, providing great feedback and encouragement. Writing wouldn't be so much fun without you. Thanks to Affinity, Irish Dragon for the cover art, and the team of editors, readers, and publishers who continue to help me grow as a writer.

Dedication

Rhonda thanks for your patience when the urge to write hits, especially when it cuts into our time together.

Table of Contents

Also by Ali Spooner

Venus Rising
The Devil's Tree
Terminal Event
Shotgun Rider
The Settlement
Love's Playlist
Cowgirl Up
Twisted Lives
The Epitaph
Bailey's Run
Sugarland
Bayou Justice

Chapter One

Rain from Tropical Storm Jacob pounded the Miami streets while the residents rushed for last-minute supplies. The storm-darkened skies allowed the nightly predators an early reprieve from their daily slumber. The hunters woke ravenous and emerged from their lairs in search of prey and fresh human blood.

A lone figure stood on a hotel balcony using thermal scanning goggles to search the bustling crowds on the sidewalks below for bodies devoid of normal heat signatures. She knew from nights of surveillance that the streets of this section of Miami were home to at least a dozen of the frigid-bodied, blood seekers. She expected that tonight she would find the prey she sought. The horrid weather had no effect on their bodies, or their abilities to hunt the living. Nor did it hamper her skills. Her eyes found what they were looking for—a body registering fifty degrees.

"Hmmph, found ya."

†

Winona "Win" Weston fished a pack of Marlboro Lights from the pocket of her knee-length, all-weather coat, and flipped open the top to tap out a cigarette. The snap of her Zippo lighter broke the silence on the balcony when she lit the cigarette and took in a lungful of smoke.

"You know that shit is going to kill you one day," a deep voice commented from inside the bedroom.

Win smiled. "Only if I live long enough." She waved away the plume of exhaled smoke and turned to peer inside the room.

From the shadows of the darkened room, a large figure approached the balcony. Dressed identically to Win, the dark-clad watcher, a woman with piercing amber eyes stepped out onto the balcony. Alix's size dwarfed the smaller watcher who turned at her approach.

The rain pelted off Alix Augustus, a steam cloud forming an aura around her figure. Her werecat metabolism, which raised her body temperature at least ten degrees above a normal human level, would prevent her from becoming chilled on a night like tonight. She smiled, thinking that her partner Win might benefit from the added heat if her smaller, human form required rapid warming.

"Damn, you're smoking hot," Win teased.

Alix knew that her figure was glowing bright red in Win's goggles.

"I bet you say that to all the girls." She peered out across the balcony. "A great night for a hunt," she added.

A feisty human with exceptional fighting skills, Win was a bounty hunter along with Alix, a werecat with tremendous strength and hunting abilities. Together, they had become an excellent team. Their skills and years of experience made them perfect hunters for all manner of supernatural creatures. Partners and lovers for five years, they had learned quickly that once they bonded it enhanced their ability to hunt together, each knowing what the other's reaction would be during combat. Their reputation as an efficient killing team grew and had spread throughout the supernatural world, and they rapidly became the most sought after team of elite assassins in the United States.

Such was their mission in Miami. King Renaldo, the eldest of the Miami vampires, had contacted them to dispose of two undisciplined rogue vamps whose careless hunting habits were drawing unwanted attention that threatened exposure of Renaldo's clan. The Vampire Laws prevented vamps from killing one another unless it was in an all-out war. The two rogues plaguing Miami were merely a tiresome distraction, so Renaldo had contracted the bounty hunters to exterminate them.

†

Alix and Win had no problem killing rogues, whether vampires or any other type of supernatural being, when there was a bounty on their head. They were both born to hunt and relished the adrenalin rush they got from the danger of tracking and exterminating dangerous supernatural beings. Alix especially despised rogue vampires. One of them had destroyed her family, leaving her orphaned as a toddler.

Alix and Win had tracked the feeding patterns of Jimmy Juice and Ricardo for three nights. In hindsight, the two young vampires should never have been allowed to turn. They lacked the discipline to keep themselves, and the clan, safe from exposure. Renaldo was paying the bounty hunters handsomely for their services, and after tonight, the two rogues would no longer be a threat to him or his clan.

Alix growled, her keen sense of smell alerted her to the rogues' approach. She despised the reeking scent of the undead. "Smells worse than a boatful of long dead fish," she snarled.

Win crushed out the butt of her cigarette and glanced at her watch. "Right on time." She grinned. "At least they're predictable."

They knew from previous surveillance that the two vamps would turn left at the next block and wait in a small park for unsuspecting victims to rush toward a parked car, or to catch a nearby bus to escape the weather.

"Are you ready?" Alix asked.

Win double-checked her weapons and nodded. "Let's do this and then go someplace where it's not raining." She grinned and a shiver from the dampness began seeping into her bones. "I get the bigger one again, right?"

"You always get the big ones," Alix groaned.

"That's because they always underestimate my size. They see you and know you'll be a brute to kill," she teased.

"All right, Win, you can have the big one just this once more." Alix winked. "You really need to work on picking on someone more your size though."

Win chuckled when they left the room. Their bags were packed and left on the bed. Once the job was complete, they would retrieve their belongings, drive to South Beach to collect their fees from Renaldo, and then make a beeline north to escape the approaching storm.

Bypassing the elevator, they made for the stairwell, the four flights of stairs warming up their muscles for the impending battle. Win kicked open the heavy metal exterior door and they stepped out into the pouring rain. Still wearing the unusual goggles, she watched while their prey turned ahead of them to approach the park, and then separated to hunt.

"You get the right side of the park."

Alix grinned, and they went in separate directions. The right side was darker, and had landscaping that would allow her to undress and shift undetected into the form of a sleek black panther.

Win stalked the larger of the pair, her heartbeat steady and strong. She slipped her right hand into a compartment of her cargo pants to grasp the handle of a specially equipped revolver. Instead of bullets, the chambers held six sharpened wooden bolts. That would be her weapon of first choice, but if necessary, she would draw the silver-bladed sword strapped across her back, concealed by her dark coat. She looked to her right to see that Alix had completed her shift and was silently stalking the vamp. She would need no manmade weapons, just her razor sharp teeth and claws to tear the vamp to pieces, removing his head from his body if necessary.

Win's prey sensed her approach, and spun on his heels to face her with a hiss, baring his pointed canines when he saw the revolver loaded with bolts.

"I can hear your heart pounding," he sneered.

She released the first bolt from her revolver, but the vamp known as Jimmy Juice easily dodged its flight.

"You have to do better than that, hunter," he hissed and began running toward her in a blur of movement.

"I'm just getting warmed up," she growled back at him.

Win released three more bolts in a pattern she knew

would cover his approach and then drew her sword. The third bolt caught him in the left shoulder after he dodged the first two, and he howled in pain when he reached for it. A fierce cry from off to his right froze his movement briefly. He realized his partner was also under attack, and the hesitation allowed Win to swing the shining blade and separate his head from his shoulders. She watched his body collapse to the ground and burst into flames, leaving only the wooden bolt untouched. A smile of victory crossed her face.

She had learned early in her career to soak the bolts in holy water for the extra pain effect, and to protect them from incineration when the vamp's body disintegrated into ash. She stopped long enough to retrieve the bolt then rushed to Alix's aid.

She aimed the revolver and, without hesitation, released a shot, sending a bolt into Ricardo's heart. Win waited for his body to complete his unholy cremation before collecting the bolt, which she tucked into a pocket inside her jacket.

Turning to Alix, she saw the big cat wiping the fresh blood from her face with large paws, and waited until she shifted back into her human form.

"I think we're done here. I'll get the car and meet you at the back door if you'll collect our bags," Win requested.

Alix stood and stretched, willing away the discomfort she felt while waiting for her remaining muscles to shift back into place then nodded her agreement. She walked back to collect her clothing and returned to Win.

As Alix dressed, Win admired the beautiful naked form of the woman she loved. Alix saw her watching and the desire smoldering in her lover's eyes. "See something you like?"

"Oh most definitely," Win answered.

They swiftly jogged back through the rain-soaked darkness to the hotel to finish their work. They were both fully aware that one of Renaldo's generals had followed them and would report to him the rogues' destruction. Win would also present him with the two bolts, which would still hold the scent of the recently deceased vamps, for further proof when they arrived to receive their payment.

They caught a glimpse of Renaldo's general before he disappeared in the shadows when they reached the hotel.

✝

Alix took the stairs two steps at a time up to their room. She opened the doorway from the stairwell and the hackles on the back of her neck rose in full alert when she sensed another supernatural being in the hallway ahead. She determined by the scent that another vampire was present and stepped out of the stairwell with caution. She could shift more quickly than most of her kind, but if the vamp were close, and aggressive, she would have to rely on her power and agility to ward off an attack.

There was no one in sight so she rushed to the room to gather their bags. When she opened the door to step back into the hallway, a small female vamp lunged at her. The dark circles around the woman's eyes betrayed her hunger and her weakened reflexes. Alix thrust out her right hand, catching the vamp by the neck and lifting her off the floor, then slamming her into the wall of the hallway before moving quickly to the stairwell. Still carrying the stunned vamp like a rag doll, Alix rushed down the stairs, kicked open the exit door, and stepped into the darkness.

†

Win retrieved the black Yukon from the parking lot and drove to the back door to wait for Alix. She put the heavy SUV in Park and emerged to run around to the passenger side. Her partner had much better eyesight at night, especially in this weather, so Win would concede her dominance to allow Alix to drive.

The door slammed open, and when Win looked up, she saw what Alix was carrying. Jumping out of the passenger seat, she drew her revolver in a smooth motion. She pulled the trigger while Alix held the vamp, who was struggling for release, at an arm's length away.

After the bolt struck true, Alix dropped the vamp as she began smoldering and then burst into flame.

"That was a nasty little surprise." Alix bent down to retrieve the bolt from the pile of scorched clothing.

"Let's get going before anyone else shows themselves." Win tucked the third bolt in her coat.

"You'll get no argument from me." Alix tossed the bags in the backseat and slipped in behind the wheel.

"Let's go to South Beach to collect, and then drive up the west coast so we can hopefully bypass this rain."

"Can we find a drive-through somewhere along the way afterward? I'm starving."

Win smiled at her lover. "Yes, we will find a spot to feed that beast of yours."

Alix growled her pleasure and then she put the SUV in gear and followed the GPS directions to Renaldo's South Beach home.

†

The streets of south Florida were beginning to look like a ghost town. Business owners were closing up shop and heading for higher ground before the storm intensified. Hurricane Andrew had taught them all a brutal lesson when it devastated nearby areas in 1992, causing billions in damages and claiming sixty-seven lives.

When they reached Renaldo's home, they pulled into the large circular drive and parked. Two huge men greeted Alix and Win at the front door and ushered them inside.

"King Renaldo is waiting for you in the parlor," one of the men stated, pointing to large double doors.

Win did not expect an ambush from someone respected like King Renaldo, but she had reloaded her revolver out of habit. The weight of it on her thigh gave her a sense of security, and her hand remained close until they stepped inside to find Renaldo waiting for them alone.

"Welcome back, ladies. My sources have informed me your contract was completed tonight," he reported with a charming smile. "May I offer you something to drink?"

"Do you have bourbon?" Win asked.

"But of course." Renaldo drifted more than walked to an elegant bar. "For two?" he asked, looking at Alix.

"That would be fine," Alix, answered.

"I brought the bolts if you need further proof," Win offered.

"Not necessary. Rafael witnessed the execution of the two rogues, and then the third waiting for you at the hotel." He poured two glasses halfway full with caramel-colored bourbon and handed one to each of the women.

"Thanks," Win replied and Alix nodded her appreciation.

Renaldo returned to the bar and picked up a large envelope that he handed to Win.

She took a sip of the bourbon before handing Alix the envelope.

"You won't even check it?" he asked.

"No need. I checked my account on the drive here and saw that fifty thousand had been deposited into the account like we agreed. Besides, I know where you live," Win added with a deadly look.

Renaldo smiled. "The envelope holds the receipt for the transfer, the ten thousand in cash to cover your travel expenses, and a small bonus of appreciation for your excellent work."

"That's always a nice surprise." Win smiled. "Thank you."

"So where are you off to next?" he asked.

"We've been requested to visit New Orleans, to help Lord Jordan out with a minor problem," Win told him.

Renaldo grinned. "Please give my regards to my friend and remind him to come visit me, if you will."

"Consider it done." Win slammed back the rest of the bourbon.

"One more for the road?" he asked.

"Thanks, but no, we have a long drive ahead of us tonight."

"Be safe then, and like always, it was a pleasure doing business with you." He extended a cold hand to Win.

She didn't hesitate to reach out to shake his hand. "You know how to reach us should you have future problems."

"I have you on speed dial." He chuckled, revealing his unsheathed canines.

They handed him the crystal glasses and turned to

leave.

"Ready to go?" Alix asked when they reached the foyer.

They stepped out into rain and a howling wind when they made a dash to the SUV.

"West across to Alligator Alley and then we'll run up the coast to Clearwater. Hopefully we can find a room," Win said. "If not, we crash in the back."

Alix handed her the envelope and started the SUV. "I think I would rather drive all night than try to sleep in this vehicle."

Win smiled at her lover. "Find someplace still open for food if you can, before we leave town. I can hear your stomach grumbling."

"I'm all in for that," Alix stated while Win programmed the GPS.

When Win opened the envelope she whistled in surprise, finding another five thousand on top of the ten agreed upon for travel expenses. "Too bad there isn't a decent steak house open, or I'd buy you the biggest steak I could."

"There's always tomorrow."

They finally found a fast-food restaurant that was the last open business in the area and drove away with a bag of twenty double cheeseburgers, French fries, and supersized drinks.

"This should hold you for an hour or two." Win removed a cheeseburger from the paper wrapping and handed it to her lover. "Don't forget to chew this one," she teased and took a burger for herself.

Two hours later, they were deep in the heart of the Everglades and heading north. The rain had begun to lessen with each passing mile and when a deer beside the road was illuminated by the SUV's headlights, Win heard Alix growl.

"Would you like to stop for a run?"

"That would be great," Alix replied.

Win glanced at the GPS. "There should be a turnoff ahead a few miles. Take it and find a safe spot to park."

"Thanks." Her amber eyes were aglow with excitement.

†

Win reclined in her seat while Alix undressed before she shifted and went for a run. She hoped her lover would scare up some wildlife to hunt and kill. Her cat needed a fresh kill to remain happy and there was no more promising area than the Florida Everglades to satisfy that hunger.

After her eyes closed, Win reflected back on her life. Delivered to a Memphis orphanage when she was an infant, she never knew or cared about her biological parents or questioned why they had abandoned her.

Her petite size had made her an easy target for larger children at the orphanage, and daily bullying became a part of her young life. When she began junior high and her size remained smaller than her peers, Win realized she needed to learn ways to protect herself. She was a fast runner but some of the boys were faster and she feared for her safety. After her school day, she worked odd jobs whenever she could to earn money. When she had the required funds, she entered a martial arts program on the campus of Memphis State.

Her instructors found her to be a motivated student and challenged her development at every potential level until she had reached the highest level of black belt possible for her age and training. When she entered high school, other students found out quickly, and for some painfully, that she was not one to be harassed or intimidated.

When she turned eighteen and graduated, Win left the orphanage that had been her home and traveled south. It did not matter where she ended up, if it was out of Memphis.

Her first major stop landed her in Jackson, and on a stormy night similar to tonight she was wandering the rain-slicked streets, munching on a burger, when she met Harley. She had stopped under the front stoop of a closed business to escape the rain for a few moments while she ate. It was the first food she had consumed all day and even though it had probably sat under a heat lamp for hours, it tasted like a gourmet meal to a starving teen.

The darkness had concealed her on the stoop and movement to her left caught her attention. A park took up the entire city block and Win strained her eyes to detect the movement. A sliver of light flashed, followed by a burst of flames, and then the most horrific smell assaulted her nose. Curious, she ate the last bite of her burger and slipped into the night to investigate.

In the center of the park she saw a dark man standing over what appeared to be a burning body. She watched with amazement when he bent down and withdrew something from the fire. She froze when the man turned and their eyes locked.

"Approach if you are a friend," he spoke.

Win, drawn to the sound of the man's voice, found her feet moving forward.

His steel-gray eyes followed her carefully while she approached. He sheathed the sword across his back, beneath a black leather coat, and Win realized that it was the moonlight flashing off his blade that she had witnessed. "Who are you?" she asked.

"My name is Harley. Who are you?"

"Win. She eyed the burning body warily. "What happened here?"

"Something too dangerous to be discussed out in the open, follow me." His eyes searched the surrounding area.

Win was amazed at how easily she followed Harley, but her instincts told her he was to be trusted. She followed him down the sidewalk, almost running to keep up with his long strides, until they reached an all-night diner, allowing him to hold the door for her while she entered the building. When she walked past him, she felt a buzz of electricity radiating from his body and she shivered with excitement.

†

Harley led her to a secluded corner booth and handed her a menu. "You look like it's been a while since you had a decent hot meal. Order what you want, and lots of it."

The server brought them both strong coffee and Harley gave her his order. "Two eggs over easy, bacon, and dry toast."

"And for you, young lady?" she asked.

"I'll take that and an order of pancakes. Some apple juice too, if you have it," Win requested. She waited for the server to leave. "You realize I don't have the money to pay for this, right?"

"Did I ask you if you had money?" he asked.

"No, you didn't."

"With the money I just made, I can afford to buy you breakfast," he told her while he leaned across the table.

She wiggled in her seat. "What are you?" she asked, "Some kind of bounty hunter?"

"You're very clever." He chuckled.

"I saw enough to know you used a sword. I presume to decapitate them based on the arc of your swing." She had a worried frown on her face while she contemplated her next sentence. "What I didn't see was how the body was set on fire."

She studied the weathered face of the man sitting across from her and judged him to be in his late forties. Win noticed he had a quick smile when she made a comment, but his eyes were what drew her the most. His steel-gray eyes appeared to look deep inside her soul when he gazed at her.

Harley started to speak, but after a quick glance beyond her, he realized the server was approaching. He waited until she placed the plates of food in front of them and returned to the counter. He began mashing up his eggs while he spoke. "Do you believe in vampires?" he asked, not looking at her.

"I've never seen one, but I guess anything is possible in this crazy world," she answered and took a bite of pancake.

"You are correct in assuming I'm a bounty hunter, but my prey is not human. I only hunt vampires, Were creatures, and witches that have caused havoc in the supernatural world by their actions," he uttered as simply as if he were describing a banking job.

Win stopped mid-chew to look into his eyes. "You're serious, aren't you?"

"Deadly serious," he answered, dredging a triangle of toast through the egg yolk. "What you witnessed tonight was the execution of a rogue vampire who has been feasting on

15

small children in the area, causing the authorities to ask some uncomfortable questions about what is going on in Jackson."

"But how did you do that?" she asked.

"I shot him first with a wooden bolt, but just missed his heart, so I had to use my sword to take his head. Once relieved of that, his body burst into flame, sending him to hell where he belongs. That Win, is what you saw."

Win did not appear shocked by his answer, which brought another of his mischievous grins to his face.

"Are you from around here?" he asked.

"Nope, just passing through," Win answered between bites.

Harley cocked his head to the side. "Headed where?"

Win stopped chewing and swallowed. "I don't really know," she admitted. "I just aged out of an orphanage in Memphis that has been my home for eighteen years."

"Have you ever been to Monroe, Louisiana?"

She chuckled when she looked up at him. "Who are you kidding? Until yesterday, I had never left the Memphis city limits."

Harley resumed sopping up the egg yolks with his toast.

Anxious to learn more about the mysterious man, she asked, "Is that where you're from?"

"I travel all over for business, but yes, that's where I call home," he replied. "What are your plans for the future?"

Win placed the coffee mug back on the table. "I thought I would travel around a bit until I find someplace I like, and where I can find a job."

"What job training have you had?"

"I've done some odd jobs, painting, cleaning, and have limited fast-food experience," she answered. Even to her ears, she felt she had little work experience to offer a potential employer.

"So what are you good at?" he asked.

Win chuckled. "Surviving," she answered. "I had to learn to fight to protect myself at the orphanage and in public school. I worked after school to pay for martial arts lessons and I can hold my own in a fight." She continued eating while she weighed her options. She had little money, very few clothes, and no means of transportation. Her instincts, which generally were spot-on, made her think she could trust Harley.

Harley liked the grit in her voice, and though she was small, he bet larger opponents frequently underestimated her. He could also imagine many left in shock by her ferocity and skills after she took them down. He decided to go for broke and come right out with an offer.

"I have an old barn that needs a fresh coat of paint and an extra room that you could stay in," he told her. "Nothing fancy, but it would get you out of the weather and fed regularly."

Win was considering his offer when he decided to sweeten the pot. "We would love to have you stay for whatever time you wish," he added.

"Who is we?" she asked, curious.

"Alix, my daughter. She's also an orphan who has lived with me since she was a toddler," he replied. "Maybe a year or two older than you, but still close to your age."

Harley saw a spark of interest when she looked up at him.

"How do I know you aren't an ax murderer or someone who will do me harm?" she asked.

Harley chuckled while he formed his answer. "I use a

sword as you've already seen, but I will not harm a human."

She thought about his answer a few more minutes while she ate, and then looked up at him. "Tell me about Alix and how she came to live with you."

Harley pushed his empty plate away and began his story. "I was contracted for a job near Jonesboro and had been tracking a rogue vamp for two days. He was killing off every Were being he encountered. His last targets were Alix's parents. When I crashed into her home, I was too late to save her parents, but I did kill the vamp before he could rip out her throat." He smiled at the memory. "She lifted her arms for me to pick her up and I couldn't resist her charms. Her parents were the last of their clan. She had no relatives to leave her with, so I brought her home with me."

"Were, as in werewolf?" she asked in disbelief.

He shook his head no. "There are plenty of werewolves around, but no, Alix is a werecat. When she grew into her teens, her first shift was into a sleek black panther."

First vampires, and now werewolves and werecats. This night is growing stranger by the minute. She studied him. There was no sign of humor or dishonesty in his face.

"What other types of Were creatures are there?" she asked with genuine curiosity.

Harley was pleased that she was showing an interest in the supernatural. "Wolves are the most predominant. Cats like Alix used to be more common, but the breed is dying out. Hunted almost to extinction for their pelts, mating pairs are rare these days. Birds, primarily large raptors, are rare, although I've heard stories about overly large eagles spotted out west. Foxes are also talked about on occasion."

"What does Alix do for work?"

"She runs our small farm, and is in training to

become my future partner."

That piqued her interest more than anything he had shared. "Would you train me?" she asked.

"I would consider it. After you finish painting the barn," he had replied with a grin.

✝

The sleek black panther slipped deeper into the night when she found a game trail leading away from the parked vehicle. She scented the fear of a small animal while her feet glided silently down the trail, and her ears picked up the distant sound of a wild pig rutting through the underbrush looking for food. *Perfect.* She began silently stalking the pig. When it came into sight, she circled slowly to remain downwind of him. Alix felt a brief pang of guilt for hunting the smaller prey and decided it would be no challenge if she attacked him while he fed, so she intentionally stepped on a branch to make a crunching sound.

The pig's keen hearing picked up the sound and his wild eyes were frantic when he turned to see the black panther twenty feet away from him. He immediately fled the underbrush in an attempt to save his life, running as fast as his short legs would carry him. The cat continued to walk slowly, giving the pig a head start to make the hunt as fair to the pig as possible.

As her pace increased, she opened her senses to track the animal. The scent of his terror made it easy to follow his trail, even though a light rain had begun to fall once more. She loped through the forest, following his trail. When he was only several feet ahead of her, she pounced. Her sharp teeth sank into his neck while her powerful legs trapped him, her grip on his neck snapping his spine and killing the pig instantly. Her teeth ached for the taste of a fresh kill and a low growl escaped her after she ripped the first mouthful of flesh from his body.

She feasted on the pig until her hunger was sated, and then located a small creek to drink the fresh, cool water and cleanse the blood from her face and paws.

Alix turned away from the creek to run back to the SUV and, for a moment, she thought Win was asleep. The big cat planted her large paws on the door and placed her face against the window glass, her heated breath fogging up the window.

†

A loud purr rattled against the window and Win turned to find large amber eyes staring at her. She rolled down the window, buried her fingers in the silky coat of the cat, scratching behind her ears. "Welcome back, my love. I hope you had a good hunt." She softly stroked the cat. Win watched the body of the cat blur when her shift began, then watched while Alix stood from a crouch, the light rain trickling down her bare skin.

Win reached into the backseat for a towel. "You better wipe down and get dressed in something dry before the clouds decide to open up again."

Alix took the offered towel. "Thanks." She quickly wiped her body down and slipped into a new set of clothes.

"How was your hunt?"

Alix's damp black hair fell into her eyes when she looked up from lacing her boots. "It was just what I needed. I killed a nice little pig that has me stuffed for now."

"Do you want me to drive for a while to let your meal settle?"

She brushed the hair out of her face. "Yeah, that would be great."

Win stepped out of the vehicle and walked around to the driver's side to slip in behind the wheel. Alix pulled a shirt over her head and took the vacant passenger seat.

Win drove back to the highway and after she turned north, the sky opened and torrential rains began to fall.

"You good to drive in this mess?" Alix asked.

"Yeah, go ahead and crash for a while. If it gets too dangerous, I'll find a safe spot to pull over until it breaks," Win told her.

Alix nodded and curled her lithe body up in the seat. It wasn't the most comfortable position for her but until her body metabolized the pig, she would rest the best way she could. She placed her hand on Win's thigh and closed her eyes.

The warmth of Alix's hand was very comforting and helped Win to relax tense nerves. The SUV cut through the dark night while Win raced to get ahead of the storm. It didn't take long for Alix to fall asleep, and start purring softly while she slept, bringing a smile to Win's face.

Chapter Two

Win drove for two hours until the rain made it impossible to see anything in front of the SUV. She slowed and took an exit, looking for a safe place to park the vehicle for a while. She pulled into a covered bank drive-through and killed the engine. She entwined her fingers with Alix's, then reclined her seat and let the sound of the rain lull her to sleep.

†

Her dreams took her back to her memories of Harley. He drove the old Ford truck out of Jackson that night, and the sun was just cresting the horizon when they reached the outskirts of Monroe. Win had slept for most of the trip, but when they entered Louisiana the joints of the old highway bridges jolted her awake.

She rubbed her sleepy eyes and looked at Harley. "Where are we?"

"Almost home," he replied, flipping on the blinker for a left turn. The drive he entered was a strip of asphalt surrounded by a canopy of trees. Once he turned off the highway all Win could see was green surrounding her.

Harley put his foot on the brake and pulled to a stop. "Would you mind grabbing the paper and mail for me?"

Win looked to her right to see a brick mailbox with a separate box for newspapers. "Sure." She stepped out of the truck and pulled out a stack of letters and magazines from the mailbox, then plucked a newspaper from the box. She climbed back into the truck and handed the mail to Harley.

"Thanks." He dropped the mail beside him on the seat and drove down the lane.

Win caught a glimpse of a white wood fence along the lane, and then a blur of movement. A large black panther paced the truck while they drove toward the farmhouse that was now visible ahead.

Harley noticed too, and when she looked at him, he nodded. "That's Alix."

"She's beautiful," Win exclaimed.

"Not bad looking as a young woman either." Harley chuckled.

He pulled the truck to a stop in front of a large faded barn. Win thought that it was going to take weeks to paint this building. Harley stepped out of the truck and the big cat reared up and placed her large paws on his shoulders while she licked his face. He laughed at her behavior and circled her neck with his long muscular arms for a hug. She stopped licking and cast her eyes on Win when she walked around the front of the truck.

Frozen by the amber eyes that stared at her with curiosity Win stopped in her tracks.

The cat looked back at him. "Go get some clothes on," he told Alix, and the cat loped off toward the house.

"Grab your backpack." He waited for Win to retrieve her belongings then she walked with him to the house.

The house, she noted, could use a fresh coat of paint. If she managed to finish the barn, she would suggest to Harley that she also paint the house.

They hadn't even made it onto the back porch when the door flew open and a tall, dark girl rushed out to meet them. "Who's this?" she asked, looking at Win.

"Alix, this is Win. She's going to paint the barn for us," he added with a chuckle.

Alix walked around Win, examining her closely. "She's kind of small, isn't she?"

Win returned her stare and almost snarled her response. "I'm plenty big enough to kick your ass."

Alix took a step back. "Such a feisty one," she teased.

"Ease up, girls, there will be plenty of time for sparring later. Right now I need some food and sleep," he told them. "Alix, will you show Win to the guest room please?"

"Sure Harley. There's fresh coffee in the pot." She held the door open for them. "Follow me," she told Win, leading her down to the hall to a pair of bedrooms. "Mine," she announced, pointing to the room on the left. "Yours." She pointed to the room on the right.

Win pushed the door open and found a room large enough to hold four girls at the orphanage. The queen-sized bed looked very inviting to her when she placed her backpack on the floor next to it.

"Is that all you have?" Alix asked.

"Yeah, I've just left an orphanage," Win told her.

Alix cocked her head to the left in the same manner Harley had looked at her. "I was an orphan too."

"That's what Harley told me. I'm sorry about your

parents."

"Thanks, but I have no memories of them. Harley is the only parent I've ever known." She leaned against the bedroom doorframe, and crossed her arms while she watched Win inspect the room.

"He seems to be pretty cool."

"I couldn't have asked for a better teacher."

Win looked out the window. "He told me he would teach me too."

"That should prove interesting." Alix growled quietly and walked down the hall.

†

Win stirred from her dreams when she sensed eyes watching her, and woke to find Alix with her back leaning against the door, watching her sleep.

"Good morning," Alix said. "Were you dreaming?"

"Yes, I was, why do you ask?"

"Because you had the most beautiful smile on your face."

Win smiled even brighter. "I was dreaming of when I first met you and Harley."

"No wonder you were smiling then. You were a cocky little shit."

"Were? I thought I still was."

Alix leaned across the seat to kiss her lover. "You're right, you still are."

"It's hard to believe he's been gone for almost a year," Win said sadly. "I've been thinking about him a great deal lately." She could see the pained look on her lover's face when she spoke.

"I have too," Alix finally admitted. "If I didn't have you I would feel so lost without him."

After more than thirty years of bounty hunting, Harley had succumbed to an aggressive form of cancer. Even though his illness was brief, he had died a painful death, and both orphans had witnessed his struggle.

During his last discussion with them on the night of his death, Harley gave them final instructions. "I've taught you all that I can. It's now up to you to carry on the business together as a team. You will become the greatest hunting pair this country has ever known," he declared with a pain-filled smile. "But even more important, you must nurture the love you have for one another. I've watched you grow into confident young women, and your love for one another is obvious. Care for each other like you have for me," he had told them.

Those had been his last words to them while they knelt beside his deathbed.

Win started the SUV, put it in gear, and reached over to take her lover's hand. Alix had shared many more memories with Harley, who had been both mother and father to her for those twenty years. For months after his death, Win could feel the hurt her lover experienced, and bringing up her dreams had opened raw feelings of loss for her. "I'm sorry," she apologized, "I shouldn't have brought that up."

"You have nothing to apologize for," Alix replied. "My grief rises to the surface in spite of my efforts to resolve it, but that doesn't mean we can't talk about him. I know you loved him too."

Win looked at her lover. "Yes, I did, but I didn't have the years with him that you did. I wish I had the magic to ease your pain, but I don't."

Alix lifted Win's hand to her lips and kissed it softly.

"Your love will be enough."

Win nodded, choking back tears from the truth of Alix's words, and pulled back into the rain to resume the drive.

✝

Just south of Crystal River, Win located a roadside diner that was open and pulled in for breakfast. The jovial woman who served them coffee made small talk while they waited for the cook to finish preparing their meals.

"Are you girls fleeing the storm?" she asked.

"We finished up business in Miami and decided to see if we could outrun the rain," Win answered.

"The entire state will be covered up with rain for the next two days according to the Weather Channel. You're going to need to head west if you want to escape it anytime soon. Jacob is supposed to move slowly up the East Coast for a week."

"That's a lot of rain," Alix declared.

"Yes, it is. We had a tornado touch down not far from here last night, so keep your eyes open during your travels."

The server filled the table with the plates of food they had ordered. She smiled when Alix attacked them with a ferocious appetite.

"What I wouldn't give for a metabolism like yours," she remarked when she refilled their coffee mugs.

Alix smiled as she cut a ham steak into smaller bites. "It's hard to pass up good cooking."

"Enjoy, ladies, and let me know if you need anything else," she told them and returned behind the counter.

Win finished her meal and relaxed in the booth to

watch Alix devour hers. "Did you see the pie slices on the counter when we walked in?"

"Yes, and I've been eyeing them between bites," Alix confessed.

"Apple or cherry?" Alix smiled and Win knew the answer.

Win beckoned their server to the table. "What else may I get you ladies?" she asked.

"I would like a slice of that cherry pie, and my ravenous friend will take two of the apple with some cheese melted on top of it, if you can."

The woman smiled. "Coming right up."

When she returned with a tray of pie, she looked at Alix. "Be careful, the cheese is still bubbling."

She placed the dishes on the table. "My father used to eat apple pie this way."

"It's the only way to enjoy apple pie, in my opinion," Alix replied, after she cut a bite.

The woman smiled. "That's exactly what he used to say." She laughed and walked away.

"Do you think you will live now?" Win teased.

Alix looked up from her pie. "I think this will hold me for a while. I still want to take you up on that steak dinner though."

"We'll have steak tonight, if we can find someplace open," Win promised.

They finished their pie and Win paid their bill and left the server a generous tip.

"Safe travels," the waitress called out to them when they left the diner.

Win tossed the keys to Alix. "Your turn to drive."

Alix plucked the keys out of the air. "Not a problem."

†

Alix drove for hours through thunderstorms and periods of high winds until they reached the panhandle where the sun was desperately trying to break through the heavy clouds. They passed through several small beach towns, and when they finally spotted a motel with a vacancy sign lit, they stopped.

Win walked inside to arrange for the room and, after paying, asked the clerk, "Where can we get a good steak around here?"

"Two miles down the road on the left is the Silver Fin," the man working the front desk told her. "Best steak and seafood around."

"Will they be open soon?"

He looked at his watch. "They open at four, which is a little over an hour from now."

"Excellent. Time enough for a shower and some clean clothes." She left the lobby.

They carried their bags up two flights of stairs to reach their room and opened the door to find a king-sized bed and the air-conditioning on full blast. Alix walked to the sliding glass door and pulled back a heavy drape to reveal a spacious balcony. "Would you look at this view?"

Win walked over to join her, and they gazed out at sugar-white sand and emerald-green water. "This is gorgeous. Why don't we spend a few days here?" she asked.

"When are we expected in New Orleans?" Alix asked.

"When we get there," Win stated, with a devilish grin.

Turning away from the view, they went back inside to shower and dress for dinner, sharing slow, sensual kisses along the way. "I know what I want for dessert," Alix said after an intense kiss.

"What's that?"

"Lots more of you," she answered and offered her hand to Win. She pulled her close for a final kiss before they left the room, and right on cue, her stomach growled loudly.

"Let's go feed that beast of yours first," Win teased.

✝

The Silver Fin was indeed open, and they were the first customers of the evening. They feasted on fried crab claws and conch chowder for appetizers. Alix was delighted to find a 32-ounce steak on the menu and ordered it rare, while Win opted for a much smaller steak and fried shrimp.

The server brought large salads and a loaf of warm brown bread with honey butter to the table. Alix cut thick slices and coated them with butter while Win gazed out the window.

"There," she cried, and pointed to the left.

Alix looked up in time to see dolphins breach the water to complete a back flip in unison. They watched the pair frolic in the water until they disappeared from view.

Alix handed Win a slice of bread and they ate their salads while they waited for the entrees to arrive.

The server brought Alix's food out first. It took both hands to carry the large platter holding the steak and a smaller plate with a loaded baked potato. "I sure hope you're hungry," the server stated when she placed the meal in front of Alix.

"No problem," Alix replied while another server brought Win's meal. Alix eyed the fried shrimp and plucked one from the plate. She moaned when she bit into the spicy shrimp. "Damn, those are good too."

"If you like spicy, you should try the firecracker shrimp appetizer next time," the server suggested.

"Why wait," Alix stated. "Bring us an order."

The server looked at the food on the table. "Sure thing." She chuckled and went to place the order.

Alix's eyes filled with excitement as she picked up a knife and fork to begin cutting her steak. She took a large bite and groaned. "Oh my God, this is heavenly," she declared.

†

The sun had slipped below the horizon when they returned to the motel, and Win suggested they take a walk on the beach.

Holding hands, they walked on the hard-packed sand and enjoyed the sound of the surf pounding the shoreline. Even though Jacob was moving up the Atlantic side of the state, the winds had reached into the Gulf, stirring up angry swells.

They had walked a half mile from the hotel boardwalk and not seen another soul. "Do you think it would be safe for a run?"

"As dark as it is, I think you would be fine," Win answered. She steered them toward a set of dunes. "I'll wait here for you," she said and took a seat in the soft sand.

"Watch out for crabs," Alix warned her as she started to undress.

"I will." She watched Alix begin her shift. No matter how many times she saw her lover in cat form, she always thought her to be beautiful, and tonight was no exception. The gorgeous black cat turned to her with amber eyes glowing and the moonlight reflecting off her ebony coat, and then spun to race down the beach. Win flipped open her box of smokes and lit one. She watched until Alix disappeared into the darkness and then raised her eyes to the heavens.

The lack of light made the stars brighter when they peeked through the clouds racing by, reminding Win of the farm. She and Alix had spent many nights sitting at the edge of the hayloft looking up at the stars. The memory made her long for those days and a return to the farm. She sighed to herself, and wrapped her arms around her legs. The cigarette burned to the filter and she dropped it to the sand. It was time to quit she thought while her eyes searched the dark night.

†

Alix ran for several miles, enjoying the scent of salt in the air. It masked the scent of other creatures, but she doubted any warm-blooded animals would roam this strip of beach. The large dinner had sated her appetite and her need to hunt, so she simply enjoyed the invigoration of the run. When she spotted a lone beach house ahead, she turned around and ran back toward Win. When she was close, she slipped between the dunes and snuck up behind her lover.

"I can sense you there," Win announced, spoiling Alix's surprise attack, so Alix, still in cat form, sat down beside her lover on the dune.

Win turned to her and wrapped her arms around her neck, nuzzling into her soft coat. She ran her hands through the silky hair and felt desire growing in her body. Alix's skin was just as soft, and Win felt it was time to take her lover to bed.

Alix turned her head to look into Win's eyes, and all she had to hear was, "Let's go," and she shifted back to human form and quickly dressed.

She took Win's hand and they rushed quickly to their room, falling into each other's arms as soon as the door locked behind them. Their clothes soon littered the floor and a naked Win walked across the room and stretched out on the bed. With a devilish grin on her face, she called out, "Here kitty, kitty."

Alix returned her smile and joined her lover on the bed. Her desire for Win burned in her stomach and stirred hormones as they surged through her body. Alix fought to keep her cat from ascending when she pounced on her lover.

Entwined, they rolled across the bed, their tongues and bodies struggling for dominance, until Alix's superior strength had Win's body pinned against the bed. Defeated, but incredibly turned on, Win tilted her head to the side in a gesture of submission, offering her neck to her lover. Alix growled softly while her tongue caressed the smooth skin and her hands roamed across Win's body, leaving a trail of burning desire in their wake.

Win may clearly have the sharper business mind, but Alix was by far the superior lover. In minutes, she had Win begging for release, yet Alix toyed with her, her tongue slipping between her silky folds to tease her lover to near madness before withdrawing to trace circles across her trembling thighs. Finally, nearing a boiling point of frustration, Win clamped her strong thighs around her lover's neck, holding Alix in place while her tongue feasted on her wetness. Win grabbed a pillow to crush into her face to muffle the scream of pleasure that ripped through her when wave after wave of orgasm left her convulsing uncontrollably.

Unable or unwilling to hold back any longer, Alix forced her body between Win's legs, and with powerful thrusts, released her passion with a feral growl of pleasure.

Win pulled Alix's face down, and their mouths locked together in a passionate kiss while their bodies undulated together, gently rocking the bed in a lover's embrace. Engorged, throbbing clits rubbed excitedly together until the lovers exploded in a simultaneous orgasm, which left them both smiling and panting for air.

Alix rolled onto the bed next to Win, purring her delight while her lover turned on her side and laid her head on her shoulder, her fingers gently caressing her sated body.

Hours later, Alix woke to find they had drifted off to sleep on top of the covers and roused Win briefly to lift the covers up over their exhausted bodies, and they slept.

Chapter Three

When the sun rose, the lovers lay still entwined in the sheets, and it was late into the morning before they climbed out of bed. Stretching, Alix walked over to peer out of the sliding glass doors to see a beautiful day awaiting them.

"Except for the rough surf, you would never know there was a storm," she stated when she turned back to Win.

"Are you okay staying for a couple more days before we move on?"

"I think we could both use some time to relax for a change. We've been working very hard."

"You don't have to twist my arm to convince me." Win picked up the phone to call the front desk to extend their stay.

Alix dug through her bag until she found a pair of cargo shorts and a pullover. "Why don't we shower, grab some breakfast, and spend some time on the beach today," she said as soon as Win hung up the phone.

Win walked over to her and wrapped her arms around Alix's waist. "I'll go anywhere with you," she promised and kissed her.

†

Alix took the keys and Win slipped into the passenger seat. She found two pairs of sunglasses in the console, handed one to Alix, and put the other on to shade her eyes from the brilliant sunlight.

They drove through the small town, noting the location of several shops Win wanted to browse through after they had eaten. They passed a few fast-food places and drove until they found one that advertised all-day breakfast. Alix found a parking spot and they walked inside to feast.

The special of the day was all-you-can-eat pancakes. Alix grinned when she saw the announcement.

"What will you ladies have?" a server asked when she approached.

"Pancakes, ham steak, hash browns, apple juice, and coffee," Alix requested.

"The all-you-can-eat pancakes?"

"Oh yes, ma'am, and I feel I must warn you, I'm hungry."

She smiled and turned to Win. "What may I get you?"

"A ham and cheese omelet, toast, apple juice, and coffee," she answered.

"I'll be right back with some coffee," the server told them, then turned to the kitchen to bark out the order.

Alix rubbed her hands together in anticipation of the meal, the mere thought of the syrupy pancakes making her mouth water. She placed a napkin in her lap and then smiled at Win.

"All set?" she teased.

"Oh yeah. I worked up an appetite last night."

"Eat well today then, because I want seconds tonight," Win stated, causing Alix to blush. "I'll even spring for another steak dinner."

"You know you don't have to bribe me, but that steak was awfully good."

"That whole meal was fantastic," Win agreed.

They were halfway into their meal when Win's phone rang. She looked at the screen to see who was calling. "Lord Jordan," she groaned.

"Let it go to voice mail for now. You can call him back after we eat," Alix replied.

Win frowned, but waited until the phone stopped ringing to continue eating.

Alix noticed she kept glancing at the phone between bites and finally told her, "Go ahead and call him back. I can't have you fretting over it all day."

Win hit the redial button and Lord Jordan answered on the second ring.

"Good morning. I hope the two of you are well."

"Yes, we're enjoying a late breakfast."

"Excellent. I will not keep you, but I need to know when you will be arriving. The situation is worse than I had imagined."

"We will be there in three days."

"Is there any way you can arrive sooner? I will double your fee."

"Let me discuss this with Alix and I'll call you later today."

"Please let me know as soon as possible."

"I will, Lord Jordan, thanks."

Win placed the phone on the table and looked up to

find Alix watching her anxiously. "What's going on?"

"Lord Jordan has offered to double our fee, if we can get there sooner."

"Things must be getting worse for him to make an offer that generous. I hate to admit it, but that's an offer too good to pass up."

Sighing, Win replied, "We'll have the rest of today, though, before we go anywhere."

"So call him and let him know we will arrive tomorrow night," Alix suggested.

Win finished her meal. Alix had ordered more pancakes, so Win stepped outside to return the call to Lord Jordan.

"Hey Lord Jordan, I've talked things over with Alix and we'll arrive tomorrow night."

"Excellent. The rogues have begun raiding our blood bank and I can't have them draining our resources."

"We'll call when we hit town, and schedule a meeting so you can bring us up to speed with what you know."

When she ended the call and returned to the table, a man was talking with Alix.

"This is Thomas," Alix said, "the cook and owner. He had to come out to meet who was eating all of his pancakes." Alix winked at Win.

"She eats like a horse. You better be thankful we're just passing through or she could eat you blind," she teased.

"Oh, I don't mind at all. I just had to see who could put away this amount of food in one sitting," he replied.

"Be careful, she's just getting warmed up."

Thomas chuckled. "I'll keep cooking however long you feel like eating."

"We hope to get some beach time, so only one more order please," Alix replied with a grin.

"Let me get a head start on it then." He walked back to the kitchen.

Alix looked at Win. "Did Lord Jordan tell you what was going on?"

"Only that someone had started raiding their blood banks."

"That's not good," she agreed. "It appears his minor problem just turned major."

Like other large vampire clans, Lord Jordan's clan ran blood banks in and around the New Orleans area as a legitimate business. The blood banks also served to supplement the clan's need for blood. They contracted with the Baton Rouge werewolf pack for blood from their cattle slaughterhouse, which they mixed with smaller portions of human blood to feed the clan. The vamps could not survive on the cattle blood alone, so their blood banks were crucial to their survival. If they could not feed on the formulated blood, Lord Jordan feared vamps would begin feeding on humans, which would be catastrophic for humans and endanger the clan's existence.

"Does he have any idea who is behind this?" Alix asked.

"We'll find out tomorrow night when we meet with him." Win sipped her coffee, lost in thought.

Thomas personally delivered the next round of pancakes. "Let me know if you change your mind and want more," he said as he set the plate in front of Alix.

"Thanks, Thomas," Alix told him with genuine appreciation.

✝

They took a long walk on the beach, but Alix could tell Win was preoccupied with thoughts of their contract in New Orleans. "Should we just pack up and drive tonight?" she finally asked.

"No, we shouldn't. Why did you ask?"

Alix lifted Win's chin with the tips of her fingers. "Because, darling, your mind is already there instead of this lovely beach. You haven't cracked a smile all afternoon."

"You're right, my love, the tone in Lord Jordan's voice has me worried. I feel there is something important he hasn't told us yet."

"I'm sure there is plenty he hasn't told us yet. That's why we have a meeting with him *tomorrow* night," Alix declared, with plenty emphasis on the word tomorrow. "Until then you should at least try to have some fun."

They had turned to begin walking back to the motel. "I tell you what. You can have your way with me the rest of the afternoon, if you can catch me; but if I win, I get to be on top." Win took off at a full run as soon as the words were out of her mouth.

Alix smiled at her lover running down the beach. If it had been dark, she could shift and catching Win would be easy, but since it was broad daylight, she would have to rely on two feet instead of four, and damn, Win was fast. She was already twenty yards ahead of her and Alix could hear her giggling while she dashed back to the motel. She took off running, slowly gaining on her lover. When she finally caught up with her, she lunged for her, but the more agile Win easily dodged her grasp. Her error, though, was moving closer to the water instead of toward the dunes. She could have easily outdistanced the heavier Alix in the thick sand, but by moving toward the water, Alix pivoted and rushed Win who was backpedaling. Win noticed the wicked grin on

Alix's face a moment too late when she dove and took both of them into the oncoming wave.

Win came to the surface sputtering. "You cheated."

Alix laughed. "How did I cheat?"

"Cats are not supposed to like water," Win teased.

"Well this one does," Alix replied. She pulled her lover in for a kiss then dunked her under the surface.

Alix noticed Win's hard nipples when she surfaced and knew it was not a chill from the water, because the water felt more like a hot tub. Win was aroused by the physical foreplay and Alix intended to take advantage of her lover's weakness. She pulled Win's body hard against her chest and pinned her wrists behind her back with one large hand while their mouths met in a crushing kiss. Her free hand slipped between their bodies to pinch her right nipple, causing Win to moan and struggle to free her body from Alix's strong embrace.

When Win broke the kiss to gasp for a breath, Alix saw the raw desire flashing in her lover's eyes. She turned her back to the shore, shielding Win's body from prying eyes while she marched them into deeper waters. When Win could no longer touch the bottom, she wrapped her legs around Alix's waist. Alix's hand stroked between Win's open legs. She could feel the heat burning against her palm when she pressed her thumb against Win's swollen clit.

"Oh hell yes," Win growled, then kissed her hungrily, thrusting her hips into Alix's hand until she convulsed with orgasm and collapsed in her arms.

Alix flashed a wicked smile when Win looked up at her. "Now we go shower so I can have my way with you," Alix teased. She backed toward the shore until Win could stand on shaky legs.

†

Inside the shower, Alix stood behind Win and reached around her to sink her fingers deep into her wetness, thrusting faster and deeper while Win's cries of pleasure increased. Her mouth pressed to Win's ear whispering heated words of passion until Win screamed and came hard against her thrusting fingers. She held Win until she stopped quivering and then gently bathed her lover.

Exhausted, Win allowed her lover to lead her to the bed. She fell asleep quickly in Alix's arms and slept until she felt Alix's firm, hot tongue sliding into her wetness and her large hands kneading her breasts.

Alix felt the wetness seeping from her own center and paused long enough to reverse her position to lower her wetness onto Win's eager mouth. Win's tongue lapped at her hungrily as Alix's lips covered Win's clit, suckling and stretching it while two of her fingers thrust into Win's wetness. When Alix felt Win quivering in pre-release, she lowered her wetness further onto Win's mouth and her body exploded with pleasure.

†

After another great dinner at the Silver Fin, Alix and Win returned to their room. They decided to lay out the clothes they planned to wear the next day and pack the rest, so they could get an early start the next morning.

Alix was repacking her bag when she ran across an item in her bag. "Damn, I forgot all about this," she stated, when she removed the box.

Win looked up from packing her bag to see Alix holding a small box. "What is it, darling?"

"I went shopping the other day in Miami while you were napping. I bought a gift for you but forgot to give it to you when all of the commotion with the storm started up," she explained.

Alix walked over to the bed and sat next to her lover. "I want you to have this for when we go hunting," she told her and handed Win the box.

Win took the gift and carefully removed the paper. She lifted the lid, smiling at Alix after seeing what was inside.

"I know you're a kickass hunter, but I would feel more comfortable if you would wear this when we hunt."

Win pulled out a braided, black leather collar with a thick band of silver stitched in between the braids, and a silver cross woven into the front.

"I know the cross is useless against vamps, but that's the way it was made. The silver, however, will provide protection."

"It's beautiful," she replied. Win took the necklace out of the box to examine it closely. She found that it tied together in the back with strong leather strips that would make it nearly impossible to tear from her neck during a fight.

Alix lifted it carefully by the edges to prevent touching the silver and helped Win place it around her neck, tying it securely before walking around to face her. "That looks good on you."

"It's very comfortable too. I promise I'll wear it whenever we hunt, if it will make you feel better."

"It will provide protection from Were and vamps, so I

will be more at ease. Witches, now they are another issue altogether, but hopefully we won't be running into any of those anytime soon."

"Thank you," Win said and leaned in to Alix in anticipation of a kiss.

Alix stepped back instead. "Um, baby, you need to take that off before I can kiss you," she reminded her.

Alix reached behind her neck to untie the leather straps and Win placed the necklace back in the box.

Alix took her in her arms for a long sensual kiss. "That is so much better," she replied with a chuckle.

Still sated from the afternoon's lovemaking, Alix and Win decided to call it an early night to rest before leaving for New Orleans in the morning.

Tomorrow would be a long day of driving, and then they would meet with Lord Jordan to discuss the contract. Until they fulfilled their contracts, Alix feared there would be little time for sleep or relaxation. She took Win in her arms, and held her until they fell asleep.

Win slipped quickly into the land of dreams, waking Alix once talking in her sleep. Alix knew they had at least six hours of driving tomorrow and Win could share her dreams with her then, if she remembered what they were. She snuggled back into Win and fell quickly back to sleep.

Chapter Four

Devin Benoit, sister of the Alpha of the Baton Rouge werewolf clan, and her lover, Tia, had been back in New Orleans for only a few days following Hurricane Irene. Lord Jordan, the eldest leader of the New Orleans clan wasted no time in summoning her for a meeting once the scent of her powers was sensed by his watchers.

Tia, a human deejay and nursing student, had recently discovered her attraction to Devin. They fled New Orleans to escape the storm and Tia had been on her way to Monroe to check on her family, racing ahead of the hurricane, when she was abducted by Cedra, a witch, and her rogue Weres.

Cedra used Tia as bait to lure Devin and her brother Damien into a fight at the Devil's Tree to avenge the death of her lover and cohort, and it was also an attempt to overtake the Baton Rouge Pack. Cedra had been the mastermind in the murder of Devin's parents and had made a pact with the devil to bargain for extra powers.

The recent encounter had allowed Devin and Damien to take revenge on Cedra for their parents' deaths and rescue

Tia from her captors. During the battle, Tia's powers as a witch became evident when she acted to protect herself and Devin from harm while they battled the rogue werewolves. Tia had surprised them all when she attacked a werewolf with fireballs projected from the palm of her hand.

Shocked by the discovery of Devin's inner wolf and her own new powers, Tia returned to the Baton Rouge compound with Devin and Damien, and was introduced to Miss Anna, an elder of their pack. Since that night in the clearing, Tia had been studying with Miss Anna, who had knowledge of witchcraft and had known Tia's Grandmother Ella, a witch, when they were young.

After Devin's injuries were treated, they traveled to Monroe to check on Tia's family and discovered Ella was the source of Tia's powers. Ella was nearing her death in a nursing facility. When she realized Tia would continue her legacy, she gave Tia her personal journal that would aid her in developing her skills and keeping the magic alive. She also transferred her powers to Tia, further draining her already depleted energy. She had two dying wishes, one for Tia to train and develop her skills as a witch. The second, she requested from Devin. She wished to have her ashes scattered at the Baton Rouge compound where she had spent time when she was a young woman.

Damien, the Alpha, offered to fund the remainder of Tia's studies to become a registered nurse. The clan's backing would allow her to focus on her education and they had agreed that she would return to the Baton Rouge pack to assist the pack's aging physician.

†

When they met with Lord Jordan, he was disappointed when he learned Tia had blood bonded with Devin, and his hopes of seducing Tia into their clan went down the drain. Tia sensed his disappointment, and brilliantly offered a proposal of her own. In exchange for knowledge about vampires, to increase her magical powers, Tia would agree to assist the clan in any way that did not violate her bond with Devin or bring harm to the Baton Rouge pack. The proposal was a win-win arrangement for both parties, and they left the meeting with plans for her to study with Marcus, Lord Jordan's second in command and the most well educated vamp in his clan.

✝

Devin and Tia settled back into life in New Orleans, their love continued to blossom, and their circle of friends continued to grow. Devin and Tia moved in together when she prepared to enter school full-time. Devin continued working with Kaitlin, the club owner and her boss, to make improvements to the club and their homes. Tia spent her days studying with Marie, a werewolf elder living in New Orleans, continuing to learn about her magical abilities. Marie was part of Devin's pack and had fallen in love with a human man. She had lived in New Orleans with her mate for fifty years and had studied magic with some of the city's most powerful witches. Her mate had passed to the other side five years earlier and she could not bear to leave their home to return to her pack.

✝

Tia had arranged to meet Marcus, to begin learning about the vampire culture, but Devin, not convinced she could trust her lover with a vampire, had insisted she tail along when they met. She would relax on the sofa while Marcus and Tia talked for hours, barely listening to the conversations until a mention of werewolves caught her attention one day.

"So, at one point in history vampires and werewolves were allies?" Tia asked.

Marcus smiled at her curiosity. "Yes, at least in Europe. Then a great war between the two species broke out over hunting boundaries, and the two have remained rivals ever since."

Devin scoffed at his comment. "Most would say we are arch enemies, and yet we still manage to do business together."

Tia turned to look at her lover, surprised by her comment. "What kind of business?"

"The Baton Rouge pack has a slaughter house, where we capture and store the bovine blood to sell to Lord Jordan's clan. They use the blood to mix with human blood they collect through blood banks to feed the clan." She looked at Marcus. "They cannot survive on the bovine blood alone, but a clan this size would be very obvious if they only fed on human blood."

Marcus smiled at Devin. "She is correct. We taint the bovine blood with just enough human blood to quell our blood lust."

"So you don't feed on live humans?" Tia asked.

"Only on very rare occasion," he answered. "Lord Jordan frowns upon the practice and those violating his mandate to abstain from fresh human blood are severely punished."

Devin chuckled at his comment. "That usually means they find themselves locked out of their lairs when the sun rises."

Marcus leaned back in his chair. "That is one form of punishment but there are others."

"Would you care to elaborate?" Tia asked.

"Not at this time," Marcus answered.

"How long have vampires been in the United States?"

"Since long before they were united. New Orleans was just one of the port cities that attracted our kind, and the active slave trading in the south provided ample food sources for our ancestors. They used the African slaves for much more than field labor," he added with a devilish grin.

The delight he displayed regarding the exploitation of the enslaved people was all Devin needed to convince her that she did not care for Marcus, or any of his clan. However, he was providing a good education to Tia that would be a benefit in her training to expand her magic, and Devin decided she could tolerate his arrogance for Tia's sake. She was always relieved though, when their session ended and they could step back out into the sunshine, and the living world.

✝

Win and Alix stopped in for an early breakfast at Thomas's place before hitting the road. Even though she was hungry, Alix stopped after the second large serving of pancakes so they could start the long journey to New Orleans.

"If you come back this way in the future, please stop in," Thomas told them when they were finished.

Alix smiled at him when she paid the bill. "I can guarantee we will."

†

Alix started out driving and once they made it onto the Interstate heading west, she turned to Win, who was reclined back in her seat. "What were you dreaming about last night?"

"How do you know I was dreaming?"

Alix grinned at her. "Because you woke me talking in your sleep."

Win chuckled. "I was dreaming of our training with Harley and the first time he allowed us to spar."

Alix too remembered those days fondly in spite of the scrapes and bruises they had given to one another. "No wonder you were smiling. We should spar more often."

"We have gotten out of the habit, haven't we?"

Alix checked the rearview mirror, and looked over at Win. "Yeah we have, we've been too busy chasing the bad guys."

Win turned in her seat to face Alix. "Why don't we plan on spending some time up at the farm after we finish in New Orleans?"

It had been over a month since they had stopped in to check on the farm. Lynn, the woman they had hired to manage the small property, was doing an excellent job, but they both missed the serenity of their home. "Yeah, somebody still needs to finish painting the barn," Alix teased.

Win smirked. "I never did get it finished, did I?"

"No, and the paint on the outside of the house has probably curled up by now. Maybe we should take some time off to take care of the farm for a while and let Lynn have a break."

"I'm sure she would enjoy that."

They had a nice nest egg established and could go for quite some time before they actually needed to work, but just when they thought business was slowing down there would be a rash of emergencies and they would be called away.

"Maybe we should even recruit and train some new hunters," Alix suggested.

"There doesn't seem to be any lack for work, does there?"

Alix reached over to softly stroke Win's cheek. "No, and it might be nice to be able to put in a day's work at the farm and then sit by the fire without worrying who was creeping up behind you."

Win contemplated Alix's suggestions while they drove down the Interstate. The idea certainly had merits, but she wondered how long it would take before they became bored and hungered for the thrill of the hunt. Not long, she suspected, but it could still be their dream.

†

Lucia, a close friend of Devin's and a Were from the Houma Pack studying medicine, helped Devin finish the final painting at the club while Tia burned some tracks for them to use when she started back to college. The beginning of the new term was approaching and she was excited about attending nursing school full-time.

Lucia was cleaning the last of the paintbrushes when she looked at Devin. "You know what time it is?"

"About one, I think," Devin answered with a grin.

"I think it's time for us to take a break and go for a ride."

Devin grinned at her friend. "Where would you like to go today?"

"I think it's time for you and Tia to see my home."

Tia looked up from her mixer. "Houma?" she asked.

"What do you think? We have plenty of time before you need to be back here for work."

Kaitlin emerged from the stock room where she had been inventorying supplies. "I think you should go. You've been working hard here and could do with some wind in your hair."

"Would you like to go too?" Lucia asked.

"Like to, yes, but I need a nap. I don't have the energy you young folks have. Let's lock up and we can walk home to get your motorcycles."

†

It had been a long time since Devin had visited another pack's compound, and she was certain Tia had never visited anywhere but their home pack. She was eager to meet Lucia's pack and her steps grew lighter while they walked home.

They pulled their bikes out of the garage and followed Lucia who made her way quickly out of the city. Kaitlin was right, the wind in her hair felt good to Devin, and the warm sun on her face was a welcome reprieve from the gloomy days of the storm. She glanced to her right to look at Tia who rode beside her while they followed Lucia down winding country roads, cutting through bayous and small towns until they reached a fork in the road and turned left toward the coast.

✝

Another half mile down the road, Lucia turned left again onto a smaller paved road. There were no signs, but Devin thought they were close to the Houma Reservation based on the appearance of the children playing in the yards they rode past. At first glance, they could almost be mistaken for Were offspring, their dark skin and hair aglow in the sunlight, but the darkness of their eyes gave away their Native American heritage. She smiled and waved at one of the children who had stopped to stare at the three loud bikes.

After ten more minutes on the road, Lucia began to slow her bike and then turned into a long lane covered by a canopy of oak trees lining the path. The lane led into the compound, and as they rode, Devin began seeing signs of the pack businesses. Several of the pack farmed and processed crawfish and alligator meat according to their advertising signs. Other small storefronts and shops encompassed a nearly self-sufficient village.

Lucia pulled up in front of a small white building and shut off her motor. Devin looked at the sign on the building and smiled. Lucia had told her that she was studying medicine to replace the pack's physician when he retired, but what she didn't say was that he was her father.

A man had stepped outside when he heard the motorcycles approach and he smiled broadly at Lucia.

"What a pleasant surprise," he cried and he hugged her tightly.

"Hello, Father." She kissed his cheek. "I want you to meet some of my friends from New Orleans."

Devin and Tia had also dismounted their bikes and were approaching the pair. "This big goof is Devin, from the Baton Rouge pack."

He offered Devin his hand. "Bradley Martin. I've heard a lot about you and your exploits and I met your brother Damien a few years ago." He turned to Tia. "This lovely creature must be Tia. Welcome to Houma."

"Thank you," she answered sweetly.

"Come inside. Your mama just brought me a late lunch." He held the door open for them to enter.

"Hey, Mama."

"Oh, dear," the woman cried, when she saw Lucia. "I would have brought more food if I had known you were coming," she apologized.

"No problem, ma'am, we'll find something on our ride back to New Orleans," Devin assured her.

"Actually, I thought we would make a stop at T John's for some mudbugs," Lucia said. "They're the best in the area," she said to Devin and Tia.

"They are really good and he cooks them any way you want them," Lucia's mother added.

Devin smiled, never wanting for a healthy appetite. "I never pass on a good boil."

"So what brings you gals down this way?" Lucia's father asked.

"We needed some fresh air and a ride in the country," Lucia answered. "I also thought it was time for Devin and Tia to meet you two."

Lucy, Lucia's mother, smiled at them. "We have heard so much about you from Lucia. Can you stay for the night?"

"I'm afraid not this trip, ma'am. I have to go to work tonight, but thanks for the offer," Devin answered.

"Well, maybe when you have a holiday or a long weekend, Lucia can bring you home and we'll do it up right."

"That would be great," Tia answered.

"Lucia tells us that you're a spell binder," Bradley stated.

"If that is a politically correct term for a witch, then yes," Tia replied with a chuckle. She considered his words for a few seconds. "Spell binder, I like that."

"Witch just seems so stereotypical and you are anything but that," Lucia replied.

"That's true. I haven't found a wart on her yet and I have never seen her ride a broom," Devin joked, causing them all to laugh.

"I can't reveal all my powers," Tia said coyly when they stopped laughing.

Bradley looked at Devin. "I also hear you're blood bonded."

Devin blushed. "Yes, that's correct."

"A very interesting pairing," he commented. "Are things going well for you two as mates?"

"Father!" Lucia cried out at his boldness.

"You have to forgive me," he said. "I was just curious."

Tia placed her hand on his arm. "That's quite alright. She's a real brute, but I love her dearly," she teased while she shot a wink to Devin.

Devin chuckled. "The pairing is going well. I haven't howled at her yet, and to the best of my memory she hasn't turned me into a toad yet."

Bradley looked at Tia with amazement in his eyes. "You can do that?"

"I don't know. I've never tried. Should we give it a whirl?" she asked him with a wicked gleam in her eyes.

"No, that's quite alright," he answered.

"I think I had better get you two out of here before someone starts croaking," Lucia stated with a chuckle. "We'll leave our bikes here if that's okay?"

"Sure, thankfully it has been a slow day. Have fun at T Johns."

Lucia hugged him tightly. "Thanks, Dad, we will."

"Nice to meet you, sir," Devin said when he walked them to the door.

"My pleasure, young ladies," he replied and held the door for them. "See you soon."

Devin and Tia walked with Lucia through the compound and she introduced them to several of her pack members. When they reached the door of a small restaurant, the air was filled with the aroma of the spices used inside.

"You ready to get your grub on?" Lucia smiled to Devin.

"My mouth is already watering."

Lucia pulled the door open and they stepped inside. "Well look what the cat drug in," a huge man cried out from behind the counter.

"Hey T John, I brought some friends to sample one of your boils."

"Have a seat and I'll get some food going for ya. What will you have to drink?"

"Sweet tea," she answered, and both Tia and Devin agreed.

They found a seat at a well-worn picnic table covered with butcher-shop wrapping paper. Tia looked around at the few patrons. They were all so huge, she thought, while her eyes passed from man to man.

T John brought their drinks. "What can I get you ladies? I just got in a few bushels of fresh oysters and a hundred pounds of fresh shrimp."

Lucia looked at Devin. "You up for some on the half shell?"

"I love oysters," Devin replied to answer her question.

"How about three dozen for starters, and a combo boil with some of your shrimp and mudbugs?" Lucia asked T John. "By the way, cousin, these are friends of mine from New Orleans, Tia and Devin."

"Pleased to meet you, ladies," he responded with a sweet smile. "I can guarantee you won't leave here hungry." He returned to the kitchen.

A few minutes later a server brought trays filled with oysters, crackers, creamy horseradish dip, and hot sauce. "Here you go, ladies," she told them, placing the trays in the center of the table.

Tia was the first to dig in and the oyster overflowed the cracker she held. She shook a few drops of hot sauce on the oyster and popped it into her mouth. "Oh my word, these are good," she said after she moaned with pleasure.

Devin used a cocktail fork to dredge an oyster through the horseradish dip and then placed it onto the cracker. "These look great," she agreed and placed it in her mouth. After chewing she stated, "You're right, these are good."

The spices from the hot sauce and horseradish primed their taste buds for the coming feast and when the server returned, carrying a large basket of hushpuppies, she asked, "More oysters?"

Lucia grinned at Tia. "Let's go another round."

57

"Fine by me," she answered.

Devin munched on a hushpuppy while they waited for the next round of oysters. "I could make a meal of these." She took another bite.

"I'm sure you could, but would you mind sharing?" Tia teased her and she reached for the basket.

Devin drew the basket safely out of Tia's reach. "Well, okay, I guess I'll share."

"No worries," Lucia said. "They will keep bringing them as long as you want."

The door from the kitchen swung open and T John approached carrying a large bucket. "Okay ladies sit back for just a minute so I don't splash any of you." He waited until they had leaned away from the table and then he began to pour the contents of the bucket onto the middle of the table. A mound of food appeared before them.

Tia's eyes widened with surprise at the amount of food. Included with the shrimp and crawfish were ears of corn and red earth potatoes.

A server followed T John with plates and condiments. "Are you home for the weekend, Lucia?" he asked.

"No, we just needed some fresh air so we decided to ride down here," she answered.

T John pulled a chair up to the end of the table and sat. "Is college going well for you?"

"Yes, very well," she answered. "A few more years and, hopefully, I'll be back here for good."

His eyes glowed with pride while he talked. "Uncle Brad comes in and gives us an update every now and then. He's very proud of you, like we all are."

"Thanks, I appreciate the pack's support and look forward to coming home." She stabbed a potato with her fork.

The door swung open and two very hungry looking men stepped inside. T John looked up to see them enter and turned back to Lucia's group. "Enjoy the meal, ladies, and let me know if you want anything else."

"Thanks, T John," Devin answered. "This looks wonderful."

He left them with a huge smile on his face from Devin's compliment, and walked to the new customers.

Tia was busy spreading butter on the corn and potatoes while Devin went straight for a shrimp. They feasted until they had consumed the last morsel of food, leaving nothing more than empty shells on the butcher paper.

"Do we have room for dessert? T John's wife makes excellent bread pudding with bourbon sauce," Lucia told them.

"I'm game," Tia replied, and Devin nodded her agreement, eyes shining with excitement.

Lucia caught T John's attention at the counter. "Can we get three bread puddings?"

"It's on the way," he answered with a goodhearted laugh.

Tia's eyes lit up when the server brought huge portions of bread pudding to the table. "This isn't dessert; this is another feast in itself!"

Devin took a bite. "Trust me I'll take care of anything you can't handle."

"Who said anything about not eating it all?" Tia replied with a smirk. She jumped when the cell phone vibrated on her hip and she pulled it out to find a text from Marcus. She read it and looked up at Devin. "Lord Jordan wants to meet with us at six. Marcus says it's urgent."

Devin looked at her watch. "That's doable."

Tia answered the text and dove back in to the bread pudding with gusto. "I wonder what Lord Jordan wants?"

Devin lifted another bite of bread pudding to her mouth. "You'll find out soon enough." She knew her lover's curiosity would eat at her until they arrived at Lord Jordan's estate. Devin was also secretly worried about what he might be asking of her. He hadn't summoned her since their first meeting and she thought it strange timing.

T John refused to let them pay for anything. "You can buy the next time," he told them. "It was a pleasure meeting you, ladies, and I hope you return soon."

"You can count on it," Tia answered wiping the last of the bourbon sauce from her lips. "That was a fantastic meal."

They walked back to their bikes and, after a good-bye to Lucia's parents, mounted for the drive back to New Orleans.

†

Lucia led them back at a quicker pace, aware of the time of their meeting. Much to the delight of Devin, she was able to relish the fresh air while it caressed her face as they raced through tight curves and accelerated on open stretches. The exhilaration of the ride had her adrenalin pumping through her veins and she was disappointed when they arrived at the bridge to cross the Mississippi River to enter New Orleans.

They pulled over just across the bridge.

"I'll see you two later at the club, right?" Lucia asked.

"Just as soon as we can get there," Tia answered.

60

"Be safe then," she said and pulled back onto the road.

"You all set?" Devin asked.

"Let's do this," Tia replied.

"You lead then. I get a great view of your backside that way."

"Only if you can keep up," Tia hollered and accelerated quickly.

Devin smiled and followed her onto the road and into the Garden District.

Chapter Five

Win dropped her bag onto the floor of the suite Lord Jordan had rented for them and fell back onto the king-sized bed, relishing the chill of the room compared to the oppressive heat that had swallowed them up when they had climbed from the SUV. Alix had followed her into the room, placed her bag on the luggage rack, and then stretched out on the bed next to her lover.

She breathed deeply of Win's scent. No matter where they traveled together, Alix would always feel at home while she breathed in the comforting smell of her lover. She reached over, took Win's hand, and brought it to her lips, delivering a soft kiss to each knuckle. "I know we have to leave soon to meet Lord Jordan, but I wanted you to know how much I love you," she stated as she turned on her side to face Win.

Win searched her lover's eyes. Alix was a formidable opponent on the battlefield, but the moments she allowed the sensitive part of her show always had a way of taking Win's breath away. "I love you too, more every day," she responded, and leaned in to kiss Alix.

Alix's eyes sparkled when the kiss ended. "I hope we have the chance to put this nice bed to use while we're here." She wore a devilish grin.

"We will, I promise, even if it has to be after this job is done. We are taking a few days to ourselves and then we will head up to the farm. No cell phones, no text messaging, just time for us."

"I'm looking forward to that. Let's go find out what Lord Jordan has in store for us." She offered her hand to Win, and pulled her lover up from the bed. "Then we get some food." Alix smiled.

"Anything your little heart desires, my love," Win teased. "Do you want me to drive?"

"Be my guest," Alix replied, tossing her the keys.

†

Devin pulled her bike next to Tia's and killed the engine. The massive size of Lord Jordan's home loomed ahead of them when they dismounted the bikes and walked to the front door. The hair on the nape of Devin's neck rose and her skin tingled when they approached the door. The nearness of so many vampires made her uneasy, but Lord Jordan had assured them of their safety, and no one would cross him on his home turf.

One of his large, human bodyguards opened the front door when they arrived. "Lord Jordan is waiting for you in the parlor," he told them while leading them to the large double doors.

Devin pushed the door to the dimly lit room and stepped inside ahead of Tia. Lord Jordan and Marcus were sitting on a plush sofa when they approached.

"Welcome ladies," Lord Jordan spoke while he stood to greet them. "Thank you for joining us on such short notice." He motioned them to sit.

Tia and Devin took seats directly across from the two vampires.

"I trust you have something important to share," Tia answered.

"I do indeed," he remarked. "I need the services of both of you, but we are waiting for two others to arrive." He smiled. "If you don't mind I would rather wait until they arrive before I explain my dilemma."

"May I get you something to drink?" Marcus asked.

"Do you have Gentleman Jack?" Devin asked while her eyes adjusted to the dim lighting.

Marcus smiled. "No, but we have Single Barrel."

"Even better, on the rocks please." She looked at Tia. "Make that two."

"Coming right up."

Devin's eyes followed Marcus to the bar, watching him closely while he poured their drinks. He was on his way back when a sharp knock on the door drew his attention, and he stopped to watch two women walk inside, then approached to hand her and Tia their drinks.

"Good evening ladies, what can I get you to drink?" he asked.

Devin turned to look at the women who had entered and Tia heard a low growl escape her lover when she glared at the second woman.

Tia leaned in close. "Are you okay?"

"Yeah, I didn't know a werecat would be here," she answered quietly, her eyes never leaving the woman.

"Is that a problem?"

"I'm not sure yet."

"If that's whiskey you just poured make it two more please," the smaller of the pair said.

"Hello, Lord Jordan," Alix leaned down to shake his hand.

"Greetings ladies, please join us. Win and Alix, this is Devin and Tia." He motioned with his hands to introduce the women.

Tia noticed Devin and Alix were staring at one another and she could feel the tension rising in the room. Lord Jordan obviously felt the change while he looked at both women.

"Relax ladies, I hope that after tonight you will be working together as a team." He spoke with a soft chuckle.

Devin's angry eyes shifted to him, meeting his cold stare.

"Yes, I know you are of different species, but I think you have a goal in common, to rid our community of rogue Weres. I'm getting ahead of myself though, please forgive me."

Marcus brought the glasses of whiskey and returned to his seat.

"I have a problem and I need your assistance to resolve it for me, at a handsome price I might add," Lord Jordan began.

"You didn't mention anything about partners," Win stated.

"You are correct, I didn't, but that was before I knew who we were dealing with," he answered. "Let me explain what I know."

Devin took a sip of the drink, never taking her eyes off Lord Jordan.

He turned to Win and Alix first. "Win and Alix are the best bounty hunters my money can buy," he explained, "and I have contracted with them to resolve an issue we have here in New Orleans." Then he turned to look at Devin and Tia. "Devin is also Were, and has experience with rogue werewolves and Tia, her bonded mate, is a spell binder."

Win looked at her with disbelief. "She's a witch?"

Devin fought back a snarl.

"Yes, and from all indications she will be a powerful one once she realizes all her powers," Lord Jordan added. "The information we learned today has prompted me to ask for their help. The foes we are dealing with are much more powerful than I had anticipated." He let the information sink in for a moment. "We learned a few weeks ago that someone was raiding our blood banks, jeopardizing not only our food source, but our identity. Until today we only knew that it was a vampire and three werewolves."

"You have my interest," Win said. "Who are we dealing with here?"

Marcus shifted in his chair and leaned toward them. "His name is Anthony, and until recently he was the Lord over the San Francisco clan."

"We've heard of him," Alix said.

"What happened to change that?" Tia asked, suddenly intrigued.

"He has reverted and allowed his lust for human blood to taint his wisdom. Anthony is over five hundred years old, and had a formidably sized clan in San Francisco. When he began feeding on humans and jeopardizing them, his clan turned on him, exiling him."

"How can someone that powerful be forced out of a clan?" Alix asked.

"It was bloody, many of his clan were destroyed, but

the sheer numbers overwhelmed Anthony, and he was forced to flee the area. This happened over two years ago," Marcus reported.

"So what has brought him here to New Orleans?" Devin asked.

Lord Jordan fixed Devin with his cold eyes. "The lure of a strong clan of vampires with lucrative businesses, and a transient population filled with tourists and homeless that no one would miss should they disappear." He leaned toward her and continued. "Even more importantly for you is the three Weres who support him."

"Why is that?" she asked.

"Because, we have learned that Anthony has promised them an established pack of their own for helping him with his plan," he warned. "Our business relationship with the Baton Rouge pack would make them the most logical target."

All in the room heard the growl that rumbled from deep in Devin's chest, and her hackles rose to full attention. Tia reached over and placed a hand on her lover's arm.

"Why can't we just call in Damien and the Baton Rouge pack, or even Simon from New Orleans to deal with them?" Tia asked.

"Because, unless a pack Alpha is challenged or outright war is declared, they cannot by the Law of the Council, take any action against the rogues," Win explained.

Tia looked to Devin for confirmation. "She is correct," Devin replied.

"But what about Cedra and her rogues, you were allowed to deal with them?" Tia asked.

"Because she broke Council Law by murdering my parents and kidnapping you," Devin answered.

Tia shifted uneasily in her seat. "So where do I fit into this plan of yours?"

Lord Jordan gave her a chilly smile. "You, my dear, are our only hope of defeating Anthony. Win, Alix, and Devin can destroy the three werewolves, but they cannot defeat Anthony without your help. He is simply too strong for them."

Alix and Win shared an uncomfortable look between them. "Does she have the power we need to defeat him?" Win asked.

His soft chuckle disturbed them all. "She does, but she doesn't realize it yet."

All eyes turned to look at Tia who was shocked like the rest of the group. "What do you mean?"

"You are studying with Marie here in New Orleans, am I correct?"

"Yes, I have been for weeks now."

"She will need to teach you a time binding spell," he stated. "Then you will need to practice the spell on our kind until you can cast it without hesitation. Anthony will be faster than anyone you will have ever seen."

"Time binding? What is that?" Alix asked.

Tia took the opportunity to answer the question. "It's a spell that would freeze time and motion for humans, and most supernatural creatures, but apparently it will only slow someone of Anthony's strength. Is that correct Lord Jordan?"

"You are correct, Tia. If you focus the spell on him only, you should be able to slow him enough for Win to defeat him while Devin and Alix take out the rogues."

Devin was proud of how quickly Tia was learning about her powers, and smiled at her lover.

"So, it would be suicide to attempt this without her?" Alix asked while she fixed him with burning amber eyes.

"Correct, and I would never ask that of the two best hunters we have on this continent."

"There are no other options?" Win asked.

"I would be open to anything you might suggest, but I have none to offer," Lord Jordan replied.

Win shifted in her seat to look at Tia. "I guess the ball is in your court now. Will you help us?"

Tia had known that the time would come for Lord Jordan to ask her for assistance but she had never dreamed it would come this soon. She was just beginning to realize the true depths of her powers, but knew she was far from an accomplished witch, and what Lord Jordan was asking could be lethal for the others if she failed. She turned to look at Devin who was also watching and waiting for her answer.

"What do you think, love?" she asked Devin.

"I don't doubt your abilities for one second," Devin answered with what she hoped was a confident and comforting expression.

"I have doubled the guards at the blood banks for now, but I cannot continue to lose clan every night. If you need time to make a decision, please make it quickly before we have to take more extreme measures," he requested.

"What would that be?" Devin asked.

"We would declare war with Anthony, and that will not be good for anyone in this town," he warned.

"Well then, I guess we have some talking to do tonight ladies," Win replied. "May we invite you to dinner?"

Tia looked at Devin. "Will you call Kaitlin to let her know you will be late for work?"

Devin nodded and walked from the group to make the call.

"Where would you like to eat?" Tia asked Win.

"Somewhere with good seafood and local fare, what would you suggest?"

"The Acme Oyster House on Iberville," Tia replied. "That will also put us close to work afterward."

"That sounds good to us."

Devin walked back. "We're good. Did I hear someone mention Acme?"

"Yes, we would like to treat you to dinner there," Win offered.

Devin looked at Alix. "She knows how we eat right?"

Alix chuckled. "Yeah she does, but we got a nice bonus on our last job, so we can afford it. Lead the way."

Win turned back to Lord Jordan. "I'll call you later tonight."

"Very well, thank you," he replied, and Marcus led them out of the house.

Tia noted a dark SUV parked behind their bikes. "You want to follow us?"

"Sure," Alix replied while she climbed in behind the wheel.

Tia and Devin walked to their bikes. "Are you okay with this?" Tia asked.

"Let's see what they have to say over dinner, but I don't see how we could refuse our help with so much at risk."

Tia nodded and climbed on to her bike.

Win pulled herself into the passenger seat beside Alix. "What do you think?"

"I'm not real comfortable about this job, and the risks associated with it, but this *is* what we are paid to do."

"Yes it is," Win replied while Alix pulled the SUV onto the avenue behind Devin and Tia.

✝

Well known for their oyster dishes and Cajun fare, the Acme was a favorite for locals and tourists alike. Tia had eaten there before but it would be a new experience for the rest of the group.

Their timing was perfect. The waiting line that would form around the block had not yet developed. Tia and Devin easily found a place to park the bikes, but had to wait several minutes for Alix to park down the street and for them to walk back to the restaurant.

"Welcome to the Acme," Tia said when she pulled open the door.

A host seated them, leaving menus for them to peruse. "May I get you ladies something to drink?"

"Sweet tea for me," Devin answered, and the others nodded in agreement.

"Do you have any recommendations on food?" Alix asked.

"Everything I've ever had has been great," Tia replied.

Win looked at the menu. "A round of oysters for everyone and some appetizers? Anything you don't like?"

Devin chuckled. "Nothing that's on this menu, it all looks great."

When the server arrived with their tea, Win took the lead and ordered appetizers for them. "A dozen oysters each, some Boo fries, fried crab claws, and fried crawfish."

"Very good, I will be right back with your oysters," the server replied, and left the table.

"So what do you make of Lord Jordan's dilemma?" Win asked.

Tia looked up from her menu. "It will take several days to properly learn the spell and practice it, but I think I can do it."

"I know you can," Devin stated.

The server returned with four trays of oysters and condiments, placing one in front of each of them. "I will be out with the rest of your appetizers soon."

They watched her leave the table, and began devouring the salty treats.

"How do you feel about fighting rogues, Devin?" Alix asked.

Devin smiled at her for the first time. "I have experience dealing with rogues."

"You realize it would be up to you and me to take them out while Tia and Win attack Anthony?"

"Yes, we should be able to handle three between us," Devin answered. "I've never fought beside a cat, so we would probably need practice to learn each other's moves."

"I think that would be an excellent idea," Win replied. "When we attack, I will shoot a round of bolts at the Weres and hopefully hit one or more of them, slowing them a bit, or at least causing them some pain while Tia casts her spells."

A look of concern crossed Devin's face.

"Don't worry, I'll still be able to protect Tia at the same time," Win said, reading Devin's concern.

"That must come at any cost," Alix stated. "Without her magic we are doomed to fail."

Devin let the words sink in. She realized they would be dealing with someone more powerful than Cedra the witch from Monroe that they had destroyed in Baton Rouge. Of course, then she had Damien fighting by her side, and pack members from Baton Rouge and the Monroe pack that would have backed them up if needed.

"I think we should have back up in case we fail," she suggested.

"What would you suggest?" Win asked Devin.

"It would have to be some of Lord Jordan's clan since they are the ones under attack. We should request at least two dozen of his best to be near and ready to step in should we fail. If we fail, hopefully they will be weakened enough to be defeated."

"Failure is not an option," Alix replied..

"Not one we would willingly choose, but we do need a backup plan," Tia commented, agreeing with Devin.

Alix was about to speak once more but the arrival of the server with a mound of appetizers interrupted them.

"Here you go ladies," she said. "Have you decided on your meals?"

They all nodded and Win was the first to order. "I'll have a bowl of the red beans and rice and the fried soft shell crab."

"Fries and a salad with that?" the server asked.

Win looked at the mound of boo fries on the table. "Do you have loaded baked potatoes?"

"Yes we do, so a loaded spud, and for a dressing?"

"I'd like Thousand Island," Win answered.

The server jotted notes and looked at Alix.

"I'd like the seafood platter with a loaded potato, and honey mustard. I would also like a Peace Maker Po Boy on the side."

The server's left eyebrow arched, but she wrote down the order and looked at Tia.

"Fried shrimp, a loaded potato, and ranch," she replied.

Finally, it was Devin's turn to order.

"I'd also like the seafood platter with a Peace Maker on the side, baked loaded, and honey mustard. Lots more of these hushpuppies too," she added with a grin.

"Would you ladies like me to stagger the Po Boys until you're into your meals?"

"Yes, that would be great," Devin answered.

"I have to admit these boo fries are sinful," Win told them. She scooped another portion of the messy gravy-and cheese-covered fries onto her plate.

"I could make a meal of them alone," Tia said.

"You two go right ahead with those fries and Alix and I will handle the crab claws and crawfish," Devin stated while she filled her plate.

"Oh heck no," Tia cried and she swiped a crab claw from Devin's plate. "Oh, those are good too," she moaned.

Alix stabbed two crawfish on her fork and dredged them through a spicy cocktail sauce before placing them in her mouth. "You should try these too, but not too many," she said to Tia with a wink.

"So where do you two work?" Win asked.

"I tend bar at a local club. Tia was our regular DJ, but she's leaving us to go to nursing school full time," Devin answered.

"That's a very honorable profession," Win replied.

"We hope she'll return to the Baton Rouge pack to help our Doc once she has graduated," Devin continued.

"There is no hope to it. I will be going back with you," Tia corrected her.

Win looked at Tia. "I couldn't help but notice Devin's mark on you. I take it you are blood bonded too?"

Tia pulled back the hair so they could clearly see the paw print marking her neck at the hairline.

"Yes, we are," Devin stated proudly. "She keeps me on my toes," she added with a sheepish grin.

Tia chuckled at her lover's remark. "Only because I threaten to turn her into a toad."

"That would certainly be incentive for me," Alix said with a grin to Devin.

"Not to be a spoil sport here, but what is our next move?" Win asked.

Alix grinned at them. "She's a compulsive planner, but she can't help it."

"I'll go to Marie in the morning and begin learning the spell."

"Is there a remote spot to go for a run and where we can do some sparring?" Alix asked.

"I usually run at night on the levee next to the Big Muddy. There are several open fields that should be sheltered enough to allow us to spar," Devin replied.

"Can we meet in the morning to scout the location?" Win asked.

"Sure, I'm usually up by seven," Devin answered.

"Are we in agreement this is a go then?" Alix asked.

They all nodded their approval.

"I'll call Lord Jordan tonight then, get more detail, and see if he has any idea where Anthony's lair is located. I would like to scout him out if we can."

"That sounds like a good idea," Devin said. "It would be fantastic if we could locate his lair and attack him in his weakened state during the daytime."

Alix smiled at Devin. "That would be too lucky, but we should plan for both options."

When the main course arrived, the foursome ate heartily, and between Alix and Devin, not a morsel remained of the food. The server was shocked when she returned to find the food consumed.

"Did you ladies save room for dessert?"

"Pecan cobbler for me," Tia stated.

"Bread pudding here," came from Devin.

"We'll have two Banana Foster pies, please," Win added.

"Coming right up," the server stated, while still shaking her head in amazement.

"Why don't you two follow us to the club for a nightcap?" Tia suggested. "It's not that far from here and you can meet Devin there in the morning."

"We could do that, call Lord Jordan, then go crash," Win stated.

"Done deal," Alix grinned.

Chapter Six

The club had a decent crowd when they entered, and Tia recognized some of the tracks she had burned were playing on the system. Lucia and Kaitlin were working behind the bar while George worked the door. She and Devin greeted George then led Win and Alix to the bar.

"Hey, Boss," Tia said when she slipped behind the bar.

"Hey, welcome," Kaitlin answered while Lucia eyed the newcomers.

"We would like to introduce you two to some friends of ours. Win, Alix, this is my boss Kaitlin and our friend, Lucia."

"Pleased to meet you," Kaitlin told them while Alix and Win took a seat at the bar.

"Likewise, ma'am," Alix replied, her southern manners on full strength.

"What can I get you two to drink?" Devin asked.

"Two Abita's please," Win requested.

"Coming right up."

"Lucia told me you all had a great ride this afternoon," she said to Tia.

"It was great, a nice break from the stifling heat of the city."

Kaitlin fanned herself. "I know. The humidity was horrible today."

Devin brought two Abita's and placed them on the bar. "I'm going to grab another case." She walked to the storeroom with Lucia on her heels.

"I thought you were meeting a vampire?" she whispered.

Devin chuckled. "It's a complicated story. I'll fill you in later, okay?"

"Sure, my friend," she answered. "Is that really a werecat sitting at the bar?"

Devin looked at her and smiled. "Yes, Alix is a cat, but she seems pretty cool."

"Interesting," Lucia remarked. She took a case of beer from Devin.

Devin grabbed another case and followed her back behind the bar. Tia was sitting beside Win.

"Do you want me to spin some live tunes?" Tia asked Kaitlin.

"No, you relax tonight. The crowd seems to be enjoying the tracks you've burned."

A slow song began playing. "Would you care for a spin around the dance floor?" Win asked Alix.

Alix smiled at her lover. "Can your feet take it?" she teased.

"C'mon, hot stuff," Win said, and dragged the much larger Alix to the dance floor.

Kaitlin watched them dance for a moment. "They seem pretty nice. How long have you known them?"

Devin looked at her watch. "About four hours now."
Kaitlin broke out laughing and left the bar to bus some tables.

✝

Alix breathed deeply of Win's scent and then leaned down to nuzzle her neck. Win pressed her body in close to Alix while their bodies moved in unison on the dance floor. Alix had teased her about stepping on her feet but she was a graceful dancer.

"It has been too long since we've danced," Alix said when she looked down into Win's eyes.

They glittered with passion while she looked deep into the eyes of the woman she loved. "We have a lot of catching up to do," she told her while her hand on the back of Alix's neck pulled her face down for a kiss.

Alix could hear the rush of Win's blood through her veins when the kiss deepened and her desire began to grow. The song was almost over when they broke the kiss. "I think we should finish our beers, say goodnight to our new partners, and go make good use of that nice bed." Her cat purred with approval.

"I'll call Lord Jordan on the way." Win took Alix's hand to lead her back to their seats.

✝

They chatted with Tia and Devin for a few more minutes while they finished their beer.

"We had a long drive today, so we're going to crash for the night," Alix said. "We'll meet you here in the morning at eight. Is that all right?"

"I'll be here," Devin replied. "Be safe and get some rest."

"It was nice meeting y'all," Win stated.

"Yes it was. Maybe after all of this is over we can have some fun," Tia suggested.

Win sent her a quick smile. "We'd like that. We want to spend a few extra days here before we go back to Monroe."

"I'm from Monroe," Tia stated.

"We have a little farm just on the outskirts of town," Alix told her. "You two will have to come for a visit."

"You have a deal," Devin promised.

"Goodnight then ladies," Alix told them and they left the club.

✝

The humidity met them at the door. "Geez, you would think this close to the Gulf there would at least be a little cool breeze," Win groaned.

"Better get used to it fast. It looks like we'll be here longer than planned."

Win aimed the vents from the AC directly on her and slumped back in the seat while it blew full speed. "Dial Lord Jordan on the SUV if you will, and that way we can both hear what he has to say," she requested.

Alix pressed the controls and gave the on-board phone the command to call him while the SUV idled in the parking lot of the club.

"Good evening, ladies," his cool voice came over the speakers.

"We have an agreement with Tia and Devin," Win reported. "What do you know about Anthony's whereabouts? Any idea where his lair could be?"

"I have every available scout searching each night, but the most we have learned is that they head east toward the Ninth Ward, or maybe even into Chalmette," he answered. "There are a plethora of abandoned buildings there they could be using, but that seems way below Anthony's standard."

"Could it be a diversion?" Alix asked.

"Of course. He didn't survive five hundred years by being careless even if he has lost his mind," he answered rather sharply. When he realized his tone, he was quick to apologize. "I'm sorry for sounding so short-tempered."

"No apology necessary," Win told him. "We realize how dire this situation has become for you."

"What are your plans?" he asked.

"Tia will begin learning the spell tomorrow while the rest of us will get in some sparring and scouting. Your clan is aware of our presence in the city, correct?"

Lord Jordan chuckled, a low cold sound that made Win shiver. "Yes they are. I'd hate it if you took out half of my clan while you were here."

"Thanks, just remind them to steer clear of us while we're hunting," Win stated.

Alix hit the mute button on the steering wheel and turned to Win. "Do you want to ask him about a backup force?"

"Might as well get him prepared," she answered.

Alix turned off the mute button. "Something else we discussed tonight, Lord Jordan, was having a couple dozen of your strongest fighters for backup just in case we're unsuccessful," Alix told him.

They could hear his pause while he formed his response. "I'm glad you have realized the seriousness of this threat. Marcus will begin training two dozen of our best. I would highly regret if you perished during this conflict, but if you fail, hopefully they would be weakened enough that we could finish them off."

"That's exactly what we were thinking," Win stated. "We have no intention of failing, but if it happens, at least you can defeat him before he has a chance to escape and rebuild his strength."

Lord Jordan hesitated like he wanted to say more before he continued. "Get a good night's rest then and tomorrow we shall begin. I'll keep you posted on the scouting reports."

"Very well then. Goodnight, Lord Jordan." Alix ended the call.

She put the SUV in gear and pulled slowly from the parking lot while Win was silent, lost deep in her thoughts.

"A penny for your thoughts, pretty woman."

Win turned in her seat to face her lover. "I was just wondering if we wouldn't be better off to cut our losses here and go home."

Alix chuckled at her response. "We would, but we would regret it later, and we can't afford for Anthony's strength to grow any further. Too many are already in danger, both human and Were."

Win reached over and took her hand. "I know you're right, but I can't shake the sense of doom that engulfs me when I think of this case."

The expression on Alix's face turned to worry. "Is it worse than any other time?"

"Just stronger," Win answered. "Makes me very

uneasy."

"Then we must plan better and train harder," Alix replied, and lifted Win's hand to her lips for a quick kiss.

†

Tia and Lucia took a walk outside while Kaitlin and Devin handled business at the club. Tia told her about the meeting with Lord Jordan and the imminent danger building in New Orleans. She shared with her their plan to team up with Alix and Win, the two highly trained bounty hunters, to bring Anthony and his rogues to justice before they could wreak more havoc on the city.

"Are you two always going to be getting into these kinds of messes?" Lucia asked.

Tia managed a weak smile. "Lord I hope not."

"What can I do to help?"

"You are too precious to be involved in this, but we may need you for some medical attention before this is over."

"I will do my very best," Lucia said.

"I know you will, my friend," Tia stated and hugged her. "We may also ask you to fill in for Devin at the club when we start to hunt."

"That's no problem, I like hanging out here," she replied.

Tia smiled. "I hear ya."

"C'mon let's get back inside. Just the thought of all those vamps gives me the creeps." Lucia led Tia back inside the club, her eyes cutting through the darkness while they walked.

†

After they shut the club down for the night, Kaitlin rode home on the back of Devin's bike. When they pulled their bikes into the garage, Lucia said a quick goodnight and climbed up to her apartment.

Kaitlin walked out of the garage with Tia and Devin. She surprised them by saying, "Your new friends look like a dangerous pair to be tangled up with. Is there anything I need to be aware of?"

Tia shot a look at Devin. "One day soon we need to sit down and have a serious talk, but not tonight. We're exhausted," Devin stated.

"I trust the two of you to do what's right," Kaitlin replied.

"Rest easy, you're in no danger. We would never jeopardize your safety," she added and gave Kaitlin a big hug. "Hopefully life will be back to normal soon."

Kaitlin burst out laughing. "What the hell is normal about us?"

Tia and Devin laughed along with her as they walked to their homes.

"Goodnight, Boss," Devin said.

"Goodnight, you two," Kaitlin replied, and stepped inside her home.

Tia took Devin's hand while they walked to their place. "Do you think she bought your line?"

"Not for a New York minute." Devin grinned. "We do need to have a talk with her one day soon. She deserves to know who she's involved with."

"I agree," she stated then she bumped into Devin as they walked. "Love ya."

"I love you, too."

Kaitlin entered her dark kitchen and turned to watch

the pair walk across the yard. "You two aren't fooling me for a minute," she said out loud. She chuckled then she locked the door behind her and walked eagerly to her waiting bed.

Chapter Seven

Devin woke Tia with a soft kiss. "It's time for me to meet Alix and Win," she said when Tia's eyes fluttered open with a smile.

"Already? We just lay down to sleep," she groaned, wiping her sleepy eyes.

"I know, baby, but the night passes quickly when you're snuggled in my arms. I left some ham and biscuits on the counter for you."

Tia stretched while she listened to Devin. "You are so sweet. You sure you can't climb back into bed, I would much rather have you for breakfast."

Devin chuckled at her amorous lover. "There's nothing I would rather do than spend the day in bed with you, but we have important things to do, remember?"

A frown crossed Tia's face. "I was hoping I would wake up to find it was only a nightmare." With a sigh she sat up in the bed and wrapped her arms around her knees.

Sitting down on the edge of the bed, Devin lifted Tia's chin with her fingers to look directly into her eyes. "It will turn into a nightmare if we don't resolve the situation soon."

"I know," Tia replied with a pout. "Just one more of your kisses before you go?"

Devin smiled, and leaned closer to brush her lips across Tia's for a soft kiss. Tia grabbed the back of her head and pulled her into a deeper kiss, their tongues swirling together. A low growl escaped Devin's throat when she pulled away from Tia. "You are wicked," she teased.

"Call me later to let me know what's going on with the hunt," Tia requested.

Devin shook her head. "You need to focus on Marie's lessons and not worry about anything but learning that spell. Our lives depend on it."

"I don't need a reminder of that," Tia replied, sighing deeply.

"I'll see you later," Devin promised, and walked out of the bedroom.

"Nice ass," Tia whispered as Devin walked out.

"I heard that," she hollered back from the front door and listened while Tia giggled.

Devin dropped dark sunglasses over her eyes, then she stepped out into the morning light and walked to the garage.

✝

Kaitlin was sitting at her kitchen table sipping on her third cup of coffee when Devin walked out of her apartment. She watched as she went to the garage, lifted the door, and backed out her bike. Devin started the motor to allow it to warm up, then she walked back to lower the garage door.

When she returned to straddle the bike and drive off, Kaitlin thought it strange. "She never goes anywhere without Tia hot on her tail," she spoke aloud. "This must be something serious." Worried, she listened to the sound of the motor as it disappeared.

Twenty minutes later, she saw Tia emerge from the apartment and drive off on her bike without a glance. Normally Tia would at least stop in for a "hello" and a cup of coffee. "These are strange days indeed," Kaitlin said, while a shiver passed through her body.

†

The black SUV was sitting in the parking lot when Devin arrived. She pulled up next to it and killed the engine. The driver's side window lowered to reveal Alix behind the wheel.

"Morning."

"Good morning. I hope y'all slept well," Devin said.

"Like a rock," Alix answered. "Have you eaten yet?"

"I had a snack to tide me over," Devin answered. "You hungry?"

"Always," she shot back. "We thought we could get breakfast and talk over strategy."

"Follow me then." Devin started the bike.

She led them to the Bourbon Street diner she and Tia loved. She parked and waited for Alix and Win to enter. The air conditioning hit them when they stepped in the door.

"I think I'll stay here all day and wait on you two," Win told them. "This humidity is horrible."

"Welcome to New Orleans in the summer," Devin teased.

They took a booth and a server approached. "The usual?" she asked Devin with a grin.

"Yes, ma'am," Devin answered.

"A double order of pork chops and fried eggs, over medium, crispy hash browns with onions, tea, and coffee."

Devin smiled at her. "You are an angel in disguise, Doreen."

"I wish you'd tell my old man that," she teased.

"What and reveal our little secret," Devin teased back.

"Riiight," Doreen replied with a chuckle. "What can I get you ladies?" she asked, looking at Win and Alix.

"I'll have the same, with apple juice too," Alix replied.

"I should have seen that coming," Doreen stated with a wink to Devin. "Is this your sister?"

Devin looked at her with a smile. She had not thought of it until Doreen mentioned it, but she and Alix did have certain traits in common besides their hearty appetites. With a wink to Alix, she answered. "She's my evil twin."

"Uh huh," Doreen answered blandly. "For you?" she asked Win.

"I'll be the odd duck and have just the single portion of everything," Win answered.

"Okay, let me go slaughter a couple of pigs and I'll be right back with some coffee. Iced tea and juice with your meals?"

"Yes please, Doreen," Devin answered.

Devin turned back to see both Alix and Win smiling at her. "She's quite a character," Win remarked.

"She's waited on me every time I've come in these last few months since I hit town," Devin replied.

Alix looked at her with a smile. "I've been meaning to ask you about that. Why are you here instead of with your pack in Baton Rouge?"

Devin chuckled. "My soul was missing something at the compound and I asked my Alpha for permission to go find what was missing."

"I can't believe an Alpha willingly allowed such a move from an unmated female," Alix stated.

"It helps if the Alpha is your big brother," Devin grinned.

"I take it Tia was what was missing." Alix smirked. "How did you two meet?"

"Yes, from the first time I laid eyes on her I knew she was to be mine." Devin smiled with thoughts of Tia. "My first night in New Orleans, I rode around the city and found myself standing outside a small club, thumping with music. I stepped inside and the scent of Tia overwhelmed me. Her body smells of cinnamon and apples, and a feeling of contentment came over me. After a brief confrontation with an aggressive bouncer, who later turned into a teddy bear, I struck up a conversation with the club owner, Kaitlin. By the night's end, I had a job and a place to stay, and I was delighted to find that Tia, the beautiful DJ, also lived on the property and would be my neighbor."

Devin sighed deeply before continuing her story. "There were no fireworks or sparks that flew immediately, but we were both attracted to one another. I was relatively naïve to the ways of the world, and previous lovers had destroyed Tia's trust in others." A smile crossed Devin's face. "Our fates were meant to be entwined and after the battle in the bayou with Cedra, they were sealed together when we both realized we were meant to be mates."

"You make a very handsome, albeit unique pairing,"

Alix replied.

Devin grinned back at her. "Isn't that like the pot calling the kettle black?"

"Point taken, my friend," Alix agreed with a deep chuckle.

"So how did the two of you meet?" Devin asked.

"We were both orphans. Win was dropped off at an orphanage in Memphis as a baby and I was rescued by my adopted father, Harley Augustus, from a vampire that had killed my parents," Alix told her.

Win took up the story.

"After I aged out of the orphanage, I hit the road south and met Harley in Jackson, Mississippi, while he was working a case. I was intrigued by him from the start and he offered me shelter and food for painting a barn at his farm in Monroe."

"Mind you, the barn still needs painting," Alix interjected.

Win chuckled. "Yes, I never finished painting it. Yet."

"Harley trained both of us to be bounty hunters to work with him and then we fell in love. At first, we were highly competitive with one another for Harley's praise and attention, but we soon realized we were better as a pair. Once we started working in unison, we too realized that we were perfect mates for one another." Alix chuckled at the memory. "A year after Harley brought her home, we bonded as mates."

Win opened a black leather cuff from around her wrist to show the tattoo-like mark of Alix's paw print, signifying their bond.

Devin smiled at the mark, which looked much like her own on Tia's neck.

Doreen returned, interrupting the conversation with a steaming pot of coffee and poured cups for all of them.

"Do you need help catching those pigs, Doreen?" Devin teased.

"Naw, I've got Jimmy, the short order cook, working on it."

"Did you have any problems with the storm?" she asked.

Doreen shot her a smile. "Nope, we boarded up and rode it out. Best sleep I've had in years."

Devin chuckled as Doreen walked away to serve other customers and then turned back to the pair across the table. "So what's the plan this morning?"

"We talked to Lord Jordan last night and his scouts think Anthony may be holed up in the Ninth Ward or in Chalmette, is that right, Alix?"

"Yes, it was Chalmette." She looked from Win to Devin. "We assume you can take us there?"

"I would think he was pretty desperate if he has sought safety in the Ninth Ward," Devin replied.

Win looked at her with interest. "Why is that?"

Devin knew any description she could offer to describe the devastation Hurricane Katrina had inflicted on the Lower Ninth Ward would fall short, so she decided to allow Win, and Alix to make their own assumptions. "It's too hard to describe. You'll see for yourself after breakfast."

Doreen interrupted any further conversation on the topic when she arrived with the first armload of platters.

Win's eyes grew wide when she placed a platter with three pork chops and three fried eggs with a mound of hash browns in front of her. "This is a normal order?"

"Yep," Devin replied, her eyes glowing when Doreen kept bringing plates of food and a large stack of toast, then returned for tea and juice.

"Enjoy ladies," she told them when she placed the drinks on the table. "I need a break after carrying out all of that food," she teased. "I'll be back with more coffee in a minute."

Devin looked up at her with admiration. "Take your time, we have enough here to keep us busy."

Win went to work cutting the pork chops on her platter. "We thought we would ride around and become familiar with the east side after breakfast."

"I'll take my bike back to the club after we eat then, and ride with y'all." She looked at Alix. "Maybe our 'Spidey' senses can pick up some hits."

Alix laughed, knowing that Devin was referring to the tingling sensations they experienced when other supernatural creatures were near. "I hope we get a few hits."

"What then if we do? Investigate or move on?" Devin asked.

Win chewed a bite of the meat. "We'll have to play that by ear. If it looks safe we will investigate, but we don't want to fall into any traps Anthony may have waiting for us."

"I think it would be safe to assume if we get a vamp and werewolf hit in the same area that we are on the right track," Devin stated.

Alix nodded her head while she chewed. "That's right, I don't know of many vamps who would travel in the company of mere Were's unless he had a really good reason."

"Just keep in mind this isn't any regular vamp we are talking about," Win reminded them.

Doreen returned with the coffee pot. "How is it ladies?"

"Fantastic," Alix answered, wiping egg yolk from the

corner of her mouth.

"Let me know if I can get you anything else," she told them and walked behind the counter.

Win looked at Devin with a smile. "I understand now why your clan owns a slaughter house. I can't imagine feeding a pack of Weres."

"We can go through vast amounts of food, but on the compound we supplement our meals with what we hunt for our inner selves."

Alix nearly purred at Devin's statement. "Nothing like a good hunt."

"I agree, but you will find little to hunt here in the city worth eating," Devin teased.

"When you and Tia visit us in Monroe, we will hunt together," Alix promised.

Devin smiled. "I would like that." Despite her initial misgivings about werecats, Devin found she enjoyed the company of Alix and Win.

After finishing the meal, Devin attempted to pay for the feast. "It's on us," Win replied. "Trust me, Lord Jordan will be paying for this one and many more before we're done."

Devin smiled and walked with them to the parking lot. "Follow me and I will drop my bike at the club."

†

Tia had arrived at Miss Marie's and was sitting at her kitchen table drinking coffee while she explained what Lord Jordan was asking of her.

"My child, you are getting in deep with this request. Are you sure there is no other way?"

"Not that any of us can come up with that wouldn't lead to massive bloodshed," Tia answered. "Can you teach me the spell?"

Marie chuckled. "Of course I can, but are you ready? Casting this spell will take a lot of energy from you, especially if this Anthony you speak of is a powerful vampire."

"I don't have any other choice, Marie," Tia stated.

Marie stood and walked to a kitchen cabinet and pulled down a strange looking jar. "Very well then." She dropped several grains into a cup and poured hot water over them. She carried the cup to Tia and said, "Drink this."

Tia looked into the cup at the deep green liquid. "What is this?"

"You probably don't want to know, but drink it. The taste is foul but it will help build up your energy," she promised. She walked back into the kitchen and placed a portion of the grains into a bag for Tia. She carried the bag to the table and placed it in front of Tia.

"Three times a day you will need to drink a cup. Don't miss a dose for at least the next three days," she warned.

Tia looked at her warily.

She sat next to Tia. "Drink!"

Hesitantly, Tia lifted the cup to her mouth and the foul odor wrinkled her nose.

Marie chuckled. "The taste is even worse, so get it over as fast as you can."

"Why do I think you are enjoying this?" Tia asked.

"Because I am," Marie chuckled.

Tia brought the cup to her lips and drank the mixture. She fought the urge to gag and rid her body of the horrific fluid.

"Holy shit," Tia cried when she placed the cup on the table. "That was worse than foul."

"Yes, I'm sure it was, but you will appreciate the effects when you confront Anthony, but only if you follow my instructions perfectly."

"What happens if I miss a dose?"

"Then we have to start all over," Marie said with a wicked grin.

"Oh hell no."

Tia took a drink of the strong chicory coffee and even that couldn't cut the taste of the green liquid.

"Here chew on this." Marie handed her a small green sprig. She saw Tia flinch. "Relax, it's just a sprig of mint."

Tia reluctantly placed the sprig in her mouth and chewed. Seconds later, her eyes grew wide when the mint replaced the taste in her mouth. "Thanks."

"I will send a plant home with you if you will promise to keep it watered."

"Cross my heart," Tia replied and drew an X across her chest.

"Fine then, let's get to work."

†

Devin guided Alix east past the port into the Lower Ninth Ward. Their eyes surveyed the devastation Devin could not explain earlier.

Devin could feel the tears welling up in her eyes when she remembered the television reports aired during and after Hurricane Katrina, showing the despair and devastation so many families had endured during those long days after the storm. Even five years later, block after block of abandoned and condemned houses still battled against the elements, refusing to submit to the final devastation.

Alix drove slowly through the empty streets and they passed a house with a rusted red tricycle hanging from a tree limb. She could imagine the smiling face of a toddler riding it down the sidewalk in the summer sun.

"Where are the people that lived here?" Win asked, choking back her own emotions.

"Those that survived are spread out all over the country. Some remained in the area to attempt to start over, but most could not return to face their ruined lives, and stayed with relatives or started over from scratch in other cities."

Other than an occasional dog, with bones clearly showing its failing efforts to fight off starvation, there was no other movement in the area.

Alix's knuckles turned white on the steering wheel. "You can feel the death and misery that fills the air here."

"It weighs heavy on one's soul, doesn't it?" Devin asked.

"Too heavy, what's the quickest way out of here?" Alix asked.

Devin leaned between the front seats. "Take the next right."

Alix breathed a sigh of relief at being able to escape the desolation of the Ninth Ward.

"It's more painful for you two, isn't it?" Win asked.

Devin noticed the tears in Alix's eyes when she turned to her lover. "Yes, we are more sensitive to the painful human emotions that follow devastation like that."

"I'm sorry," Win said to both of them.

"You needed to see it to experience it yourselves," Devin replied. "I have no words to adequately describe what happened there."

"I understand now," Win stated. "I agree with Lord Jordan. There are surely plenty of ghosts calling this place home, but Anthony would not be here, even in his most desperate moments."

Devin gave directions to Alix to reach the small village of Chalmette. They drove the streets searching for any signs, and then Devin guided them to the Battlefield. "This spot took a big hit from Katrina too, but they have rebuilt the visitors' building and other outbuildings," she reported.

They drove through the entire park. "I get nothing," Alix growled.

"Me neither," Devin confirmed.

"Where do we go now?" Alix asked.

"Let's head back to New Orleans," Win answered.

Alix looked into the rearview mirror and glanced at Devin in the back seat. "Is there a way around the Ninth Ward? I don't think I can do that again."

Devin nodded and gave her directions to bypass the area. Their travels brought them to Esplanade Avenue and they turned south to return to the club. They were driving through an affluent section of town, and the homes surrounded by wrought iron fences ensured the privacy of the many famous actors and musicians who made this town home. Large, ancient oak trees lined the center of the streets, casting dark shadows on the bumpy roads.

They had just passed a section of townhomes on the eastern side of the street when Devin leaned up between the seats. "Did you feel that?" she asked Alix.

"Yeah, I did. I wondered if my skin was still crawling

from the Ninth Ward though."

"Pop a U-turn up here and drive slowly if you can," Devin replied.

She continued leaning between the seats while they stared out the windshield. "There," she said, pointing to a yellow brick town home. "3214, did you feel it again?"

"Yes, I did," Alix, answered. "Definitely Were, and something else."

"Turn left, drive away from the townhouse, and pull over so we can call Lord Jordan. We need to confirm it isn't one of his," Win replied. "I also don't want Anthony or any of his Weres to sense our presence this close to them."

Alix turned left, and drove down a narrow street.

"Take a right here," Devin instructed, and Alix found a secluded spot to pull over.

Alix used the controls on the steering wheel to call Lord Jordan's number.

Devin grinned. "I definitely can't do that on my bike."

Lord Jordan answered on the third ring. "Good day, ladies."

"Hello, Lord Jordan, this is Devin, Alix, and Win," Win stated.

"Do you have news to share?"

"Possibly," Win answered. "Does any of your clan live on Esplanade Avenue? Particularly 3214? It's a yellow brick townhome."

Devin could hear the rush of blood through Win's veins while her body resonated with her excitement.

"No, we have no one that lives in that section of town. Why do you ask?"

"Both Alix and Devin sensed something supernatural

at that address. That's the first hit we've had all morning."

"Strong Were scent and something else," Alix confirmed.

"Great job, ladies," he stated. "I will have Marcus research the location and get back to you when we can."

"Thanks," Alix replied and ended the call. "Lunch anyone?"

"I thought you'd never ask," Devin said. "Straight ahead and take a right on Andry's Street."

"Where are we headed?" Win asked.

"Mama's for the best fried chicken you have ever eaten. Good food and good prices," she added with a grin.

†

"Dear God this stuff is going to kill me," Tia groaned when she drank down the next cup of the horrid tea and reached for more mint.

"No, that stuff will help keep you alive," Marie, reminded her. "When you get done with that, you can fix us a sandwich while I look up something."

Tia took the offensive cup, washed it at the sink, and then placed it in the strainer. "What kind of sandwich would you like?"

Marie chuckled. "I think turkey is all I have left. I haven't been to the store yet."

Marie sat at the table and flipped through Ella's journal. Tia's grandmother had given her the journal on her deathbed when Tia confirmed she had inherited her powers. Tia and her teachers, Marie and Anna, used the journal for a guide in her training while her powers continued to grow.

"There are chips in the pantry," Marie said, when she

100

found the entry she was looking for. "I'll take sweet tea to drink."

Tia smiled to herself and went to work making their lunch. Maybe it was her imagination, but she felt a buzzing through her body. Could the tea be working this quickly?

"The answer is yes," Marie said from the table. "The tea works very quickly."

Tia had forgotten Marie had the ability to sense her thoughts. Her smile was even brighter when she spread mayonnaise on the bread. She would have to work hard to keep her thoughts away from Devin and the love they had shared last night, to prevent Marie from picking them from her brain.

"You are going to have to do better than that, you naughty little girl," Marie teased with a chuckle.

"Damn," Tia cried out, and she was glad she had her back to Marie to hide the blush that had risen on her face. "Please teach me how to block that so Anthony doesn't read me as easy as you."

"He might find your thoughts entertaining like I do," Marie teased without looking up from the journal.

"You are a wicked woman, Marie."

She chuckled. "Yes, I know. I've been told that many times."

Tia placed a sandwich on a plate and opened the pantry for the bag of chips. She carried them to Marie and went back to open the refrigerator for the pitcher of sweet tea. "Ice?" she asked.

"No, it should be cold enough. We do need to teach you to block. This binding spell is mental not verbal. If you allow Anthony into your mind, the battle will be over quickly, and you and your friends will perish. Or worse," she added.

"What is the 'or worse' part?" she asked.

"There is no doubt your friends would be killed if defeated, but I would think Anthony wise enough to bind you to him. A witch under his control would be a great victory."

Tears filled her eyes at the suggestion she could be responsible for Devin's death. There was no way that was going to happen, she told herself. Anthony could go to hell before she would do his bidding.

"So where do we start?"

"You have to learn to control your thoughts. Devin makes you happy, but Anthony will use that like a weakness against you. Have faith that Devin will be safe in this fight and concentrate on your duty. Other than Devin, where does your strength come from?" Marie asked.

"From you and Anna," Tia answered.

"Wrong answer, think deeper. We provide you with wisdom, but where does your strength come from?"

"Ella, my strength comes from my grandmother."

"Yes, she needs to be your focal point," Marie instructed.

"Flood your mind with her memories and no one can get past those," Marie said with a grin.

Tia closed her eyes and focused on her grandmother. She could feel Marie probing her mind, but did not feel violated.

"That's a good start, but your eyes need to be open when you face Anthony. Try again."

It took several more attempts, but Tia was finally able to keep her eyes open when she blocked her mind from Marie.

"Rest now," Marie replied. "Blocking eats up your energy now, but the more you practice the easier it will be for you."

✝

Two hours and six whole chickens later, the trio left Mama's, their hunger temporarily sated, and drove back to the club. Just when they were pulling in, Lord Jordan called them back.

"Answer it on the SUV," Alix requested.

"Hello, Lord Jordan," Win greeted.

"Good afternoon, Win," he answered. "Marcus has tracked down the owner of the townhome you described. The property is in the middle of an estate war between several siblings, and a man by the name of Charles Dubois has rented the home with cash for the next three months. Before you ask, Marcus has found no record of the man, but he is still searching."

"That's quick work," Win replied. "Send him our thanks."

"Done," he said. "So what is your next move?"

"A few hours of rest, and then we will do some reconnaissance tonight to see if we can verify the place is Anthony's lair."

"Keep me posted," he requested, and clicked off.

"Will you meet us here at dark? You two can go for a run while I plan our surveillance tonight." Win asked.

"No problem," Devin stated, and left the SUV. She watched them pull away and then mounted her bike to drive the short distance home. She knew that Kaitlin would be opening the club soon and she would need to talk to her about Lucia taking her place for a few days. She looked up at Lucia's apartment, saw a light on, and climbed the stairs.

✝

Devin knocked on the door and Lucia yelled, "Come in."

Devin entered her apartment and found Lucia on the floor assembling a small table. "Hey, you need some help?"

"No, I think I've got it now, what's up?"

"I need you to fill in for me for the next three nights or so at the club."

"I'd love too. Did your day go well?"

Devin smiled at the glue running down Lucia's hand. "Easy on that glue," she teased.

"Damn," Lucia cried, and wiped the sticky glue from her hand.

"Yeah, today went well. We may have located Anthony's lair on Esplanade."

Lucia let out a soft whistle. "That's too close to here," she remarked.

Devin hadn't given it much thought, but the townhome was only ten or so blocks from their home. "Yeah, will you make sure Kaitlin makes it home safely and keep a close eye on her until this mess is over?"

"You don't even have to ask. Do you think they know about you hunting them?"

"I hope not, but keep your eyes and ears open."

"I will."

Devin turned to leave and looked at Lucia. "You sure you don't need some help?"

"Get out of here," Lucia replied with a laugh.

✝

Devin walked down the stairs and sighed deeply. She needed to talk to Kaitlin to let her know that Lucia would be filling in for her for several days, and she dreaded the task. Devin knew Kaitlin would ask some tough questions, and the last thing she wanted to do was lie to her friend and employer.

When she crossed the yard to Kaitlin's house and lifted her hand to knock, a voice rang out from inside. "C'mon in," Kaitlin hollered.

"Hey," Devin said when she stepped inside. Even before she opened her mouth, Devin felt the burn of guilt all over her face.

"Is everything alright?" Kaitlin asked.

"Tia and I have something very important going on the next few days so Lucia is going to be filling in for me at the bar," Devin told her without taking a breath.

"That's fine," Kaitlin, answered looking at her strangely. "Is there something we should talk about?"

There it was, the question Devin was dreading. She tried her best to put on a confident face. "Probably so, but the time isn't right. I swear we will tell you everything in just a few days. Please, trust me on this Kaitlin. I can't tell you more right now."

"You two aren't in any legal trouble are you?"

If only it were that simple, Devin thought. She chuckled. "No, we aren't in jeopardy of going to jail, but do you have bond money if we do?" she teased.

Kaitlin was genuinely worried and knew Devin was trying to make light of what they were doing. "I could probably scrounge up the money for one of you, but I would have to decide which one is the least amount of trouble."

"Undeniably Tia then," Devin teased.

"I'll be here when you're ready to talk to me, and fill in some of the blanks my mind is going crazy with, worrying about what you two are doing."

Devin reached out and hugged Kaitlin, pulling her close. "I'm sorry we're worrying you, but hopefully you will understand soon."

"I hope so too. The least you can do is let me know you are okay. I haven't seen Tia since she left this morning and you look dog tired."

Devin released her and smiled. "I'm going to take a nap right now and I hope Tia will be home soon."

"You two are going to make me gray before my time."

Devin felt bad for making Kaitlin worry. "I'll stop into the club later tonight if I can."

"Fine, so get some sleep. Did you eat?"

"A ton of chicken from Mama's."

"Good," Kaitlin replied, and watched her walk through the door.

✝

Devin entered her house and went straight to the bedroom. She collapsed on the bed and howled in frustration. Kaitlin deserved better than how they were treating her right now. She grabbed her cell and dialed Tia. To further her frustration, there was no answer, so she took Tia's pillow and held it to her face. She breathed in the comforting scent of her lover. "I need you," she whispered.

✝

"One more dose and you can go home for the day, but I want you back here early in the morning. You can bring beignets for our breakfast."

Tia eyed the cup filled to the rim with the nasty green liquid. She thought it would become easier to swallow, but her gag reflex had other notions. She picked up the cup and downed the contents before she had a chance to change her mind. "Damn," she groaned when she lowered the empty cup to the table.

"I was going to send some tea home with you, but on second thought, I will keep it here so I can witness you drinking it," Marie said with a sugary grin.

"You are enjoying this way too much," Tia replied before she bit into the mint.

Marie looked into her eyes. "Actually, I wish these old bones were younger so I could accompany you on this adventure."

"I wish you could too," Tia replied, "but it is too dangerous to risk you."

Marie nodded her head. "I would only be a distraction for you, but know that I will be there in spirit for you."

"Thank you, Marie."

"Now go get something to eat and a good night's rest. Tomorrow you may not leave this early. Remember to practice those words with your mind."

"I will, Marie," Tia promised, and hugged her teacher.

✝

Win pulled out black clothing to wear later and reloaded her revolver with silver-tipped bolts. Alix and Devin would shift before they arrived at Esplanade, but she would have to dress for concealment. They could not risk detection before it was time for them to go into action. She was checking her revolver a third time when Alix called out from the shower.

"The water is going to get cold if you don't get in here soon."

"I'm on my way," Win called out and placed her revolver on the bedside table.

She joined Alix for a quick shower and then they crawled into the plush bed for a few hours rest.

†

When Tia arrived home, she found Devin sleeping soundly. She stripped out of her clothes and crawled in beside her lover. Devin wrapped her arm around Tia's waist when she snuggled into her body but never woke. Devin's warmth comforted Tia, and she fell into a dreamless sleep.

Chapter Eight

The sun set too quickly for Devin's taste that night. She hated to leave the warmth and comfort she felt lying next to Tia in their bed, but she had a job to do. She dressed and slipped back into her boots, then crept quietly out of the apartment and walked the short distance to the club.

She could hear the thumping bass of the dance tune that was playing inside and was tempted to enter, but she feared it would be difficult to slip away from Kaitlin when the time came for action. She leaned against the wall of the club and waited for Alix and Win to arrive.

Her eyes lifted to the heavens when the stars began to shine. The moon was also beginning to rise and she smirked at the irony of the full moon. Her nerves were on edge. The pull of the moon on her inner beast only served to make her more jumpy. A run would be good for her, helping to burn some of the adrenalin running rampant through her veins.

Devin was relieved when the black SUV pulled into the parking lot and she slipped inside.

"Have you been waiting long?" Alix asked.

"Just a few minutes, no worries," she answered.

"Tell me how to get to the levee so we can run," Alix said. "My cat is about ready to climb some walls."

"I know that feeling."

Win turned in her seat. "How did it go for Tia today?"

Devin shrugged. "I don't know. I was asleep when she came home and climbed into the bed, and she was sleeping so peacefully when I woke, I couldn't wake her."

"Let's just hope it went well and she gets lots of rest tonight."

She smiled at Win. "Tia will be ready, that I'm sure of."

Devin guided Alix to pull the SUV into a small cluster of trees. "You'll be safe here," Devin told Win before she and Alix left the vehicle.

"Have a good run," Win wished them, and locked the doors once they shed their clothes and began to shift.

Devin couldn't resist a peek at Alix unclothed and suppressed a laugh when she turned to find Alix checking her out. "Not bad for a kitty," she teased.

"You're not a bad looking pup either," Alix answered. She grinned and her form began to blur.

The naked women disappeared from her view and Win watched while a black panther and a black and gray wolf replaced them. She heard a chuffing sound and a low growl and then the two predators took off at a full run through the woods.

†

Win relaxed back in her seat and closed her eyes while she envisioned the yellow brick townhome on

Esplanade. She visualized what she remembered about the building. Two lower windows on each side of the front door had the shades pulled tight and she remembered the upper windows were darkened as well. There was a dark alley between the homes and Win thought it might provide cover for either herself or Devin. Alix's big cat could climb one of the large oaks in the median and have an excellent vantage point of anyone leaving the townhome through the front. Alix's dark coat would make her nearly invisible in the dark. She weighed the risks of following anyone leaving the home and decided to discuss this option with Alix and Devin.

†

Devin was surprised at how easily Alix kept pace with her while they galloped down the levee for several miles. She was even more surprised when her keen sense of smell picked up the scent of game, and she led the big cat away from the levee down a narrow trail in pursuit. A pair of rabbits ran haphazardly ahead of them and, when they split taking different routes, the wolf and cat separated to chase down their prey. The rabbits would barely make a snack for the much larger predators, but the thrill of the hunt sent adrenalin running through their veins, further heightening their senses.

The wolf pounced and crushed the small rabbit between her powerful jaws. She heard a frightened squeal coming from the big cat's direction, so she too was victorious in her hunt. She sank to the ground and let her teeth and claws tear apart the small carcass while she devoured the tasty fresh meat. The rabbit's warm blood coated her muzzle and her tongue swirled out to lick her face clean. Her wolf's need to hunt was temporarily sated and she trotted back down the path in search of her companion.

The big cat pounced, tackling the wolf and they rolled across the path as they wrestled together playfully. The wolf nipped at the cat's thick tail then raced down the path to the levee at a full run. They ran back to the SUV, both panting heavily when they skidded to a halt twenty feet from the SUV.

They were not alone.

A single golden wolf walked around to the front of the SUV, his nose to the ground checking scents. There was no sign of Win in the vehicle.

A noise behind them caught their attention and they turned when Win stepped from behind a tree, her revolver drawn and on the ready. "He's been here for five minutes now," she whispered.

Devin stepped forward into the clearing to confront the wolf, followed by her two friends. When he saw her, his form began to shimmer while he shifted back to human form. A beautiful blonde man stood before them.

"Greetings, Devin of Baton Rouge. I am Simon, Alpha of the New Orleans pack." He spoke with a rich, deep voice.

Devin's wolf sat back on her haunches and began her shift. After several agonizing seconds of a rushed shift, Devin stood and stretched. "Greetings, Simon," she answered. "What has brought you out this fine evening?"

"I have received word from Lord Jordan that you were working with a pair of bounty hunters to rid him of his most recent problem," he answered. "His problem has the potential to become ours as well, and while my pack cannot be directly involved, I would like to offer any assistance we can provide."

"How did you find me here?" Devin asked, suspicious.

Simon gave her a warm smile and pointed up at the moon. "I had a very strong feeling that you would be running tonight, and I have scented you here before."

Devin's body relaxed and she began dressing. Alix and Win walked to the far side of the SUV, and Alix got dressed.

Win's eyes never left Simon and her hand firmly grasped the revolver.

"I think I have an idea of how you can help," Devin told him. "Are your clothes nearby?"

Simon chuckled. "My jeep is about a half mile down the road. I will go dress and drive down here," he answered.

"Thanks," she replied and watched him go.

She turned back to face her friends.

"What are you thinking?" Win asked.

Devin grinned. "We need to control where we confront Anthony, correct?"

"Yes, that would be to our advantage. Why?" Win asked.

Devin began pacing while she talked. "Lord Jordan has three blood banks throughout the city, right?"

"Yes, that's correct."

"If Simon and his pack heavily guard two of the three, Anthony will have no choice, except for the one we give him. Do you follow my thinking?"

Win smiled up at her. "You may be on to something."

They turned at the sound of Simon's jeep approaching and waited for him to join them.

Devin introduced Win and Alix to Simon.

"I have heard many great things about your abilities,"

he said to them. "My pack would be honored to assist you like we once helped Harley."

"You knew Harley?" Alix asked.

Simon leaned back against the SUV. "He helped us out with a problem many years ago and I will be forever in his debt. I was very sad to learn of his passing."

"He was a great man," Alix replied with pride.

"Yes, he was." Simon let the silence fall between them for several seconds. "So what can we do for you ladies?"

Devin laid out her idea for him and he listened intently.

He smiled at her plan. "If I may suggest, you leave the blood bank at the end of Canal the least guarded. It will be a much better location for your confrontation."

"It will also be closer to his lair," Win added.

Simon whipped his head around to look at her. "You've found him already?"

"We think so, we're planning some surveillance tonight to see if we can confirm our suspicions," she answered.

Simon smiled at the news. "There is a fourth to your team, correct, a spell binder?"

"Yes, she is learning a spell we hope will even our odds and improve our chance for success," Devin replied.

"This vamp, he is powerful, eh?"

"Very much so according to Lord Jordan," Win answered.

"Do you have any time frame for when you plan to confront him?" Simon asked.

"Not a solid one yet, it depends on several factors. We should plan to meet again tomorrow once we have an update. Are you comfortable meeting at Lord Jordan's home?" Devin asked.

He chuckled. "I've been his guest more than once. You know how to contact me, so give me a call once you have a meeting set up," he told Devin.

She reached out her hand. "Thanks for your help."

He shook her hand and then cocked his head. "Does Damien know what you're up to?"

"No, and I would prefer it to stay that way, Simon."

His expression turned serious. "It goes against my instinct, but I will honor your request. For now at least," he replied with a grin.

Devin relaxed. "Thanks, I don't want him to worry or break the Council's Covenants by getting involved."

"I will await your call then," Simon stated, and climbed into his Jeep and drove away.

She watched his tail lights disappear into the darkness. "That was certainly a surprise," Devin stated.

"A pleasant one though. I'm feeling better about this plan," Win replied.

"Me too," she agreed. "Let's go hunting."

They climbed into the SUV and Win told them of her plan for the evening, putting Alix up a tree while she and Devin used the concealment of an alleyway to survey the town home.

"What I need to know is what we will do if one or more of the Weres leaves the house. Do we follow, confront, or just stay in place?" Win asked.

"If one wolf goes out tonight we could easily defeat him, but we run the risk of revealing ourselves to Anthony and putting him on guard if one of his rogues disappears," Devin warned. "I would love to take one out but I think the risk is too great."

"I agree with you," Alix said.

"So we take up our positions and see what happens tonight then," Win replied.

"Let's park where we did earlier today if we can," Devin suggested. "Close but not obvious."

Alix reached down, started the SUV, and backed from their hiding spot. Devin sat back in her seat and willed her racing heart to return to normal. The last thing she needed to do was give away her position with a racing heartbeat.

†

The traffic on Esplanade was still heavy for that time of night and they hoped it would help conceal their presence from the creatures within the townhouse. Alix found the parking spot and they were lucky that the bulb in the street light had burnt or blown out, providing the darkness Alix and Devin needed to complete their transformations.

Win reached up to switch off the interior light of the SUV and looked at Devin. "Are we ready for this?"

Devin took a deep breath. "The only thing we haven't discussed is what we would do if Anthony leaves the home."

"If he leaves the house, we should do our best to remain unseen. I think it's clear that we cannot defeat him alone," Win warned while a shiver passed through her. She fought the urge to shake it from her body. Win knew she had to appear calm and fearless for her two partners. The stench of her fear would make their inner beasts uneasy. The dangers they were about to face made it critical for them to remain calm and predictable.

"Are we in agreement that if a man or wolf leaves I will follow him?" Devin asked.

"Yes, we're okay with that. Plan on meeting us back at the club, if you follow him," Win said.

Devin nodded her head and began undressing in the back seat. Alix would have to leave the SUV and walk around to undress because of the bulk of the steering wheel.

"Lock and load," Devin said to Win, when she slipped from the vehicle.

"I'll be ready if needed," Win assured her.

Devin shifted and waited for Win to join her. They watched while the sleek black panther cut through the night and dashed across the avenue to leap up into one of the giant oaks. Devin and Win waited while she located a thick branch. Devin could see Alix, concealed from normal eyesight, and only her enhanced night vision allowed her to locate the sleek panther perched in the tree.

Win whispered to Devin. "Ready?"

Devin responded by walking ahead of her in the deep shadows until they reached a spot where they could quickly cross the avenue and slip into a back alley. They moved silently and crept as close to the town house as possible. Devin lifted her nose to the breeze to find they were down wind of the townhome. She hoped the rogues were feeling overconfident, and would not become disturbed by their scents in the area. Were creatures roamed all over the city and they hoped their scents would blend with others they were used to smelling.

✝

Tia's hunger woke her around midnight and she instinctively reached over to Devin's side of the bed, only to find it cold and empty. "Where are you, my love?" she spoke aloud. She climbed from the bed and walked to the kitchen to open the refrigerator and stare at the contents.

Her stomach rumbled with the promise of food and Tia pulled out sliced ham and cheese to prepare a sandwich. It felt odd to her that she was alone. Kaitlin and Lucia were at the club and Devin was missing in action. It was the first time she could ever remember being alone on the property and she was sure she didn't like the uneasiness that settled on her shoulders.

She replaced the food in the refrigerator and poured a glass of tea and then turned the lights out in the kitchen before she sat at the table to eat her sandwich. Tia realized it was silly to be sitting in the dark. Any creature that she feared would have the eyesight to see through the darkness but she refused to turn the lights back on.

She stared out the front window while she mechanically chewed the sandwich and worried where Devin might be and wondered if she were in danger.

"Of course she's in danger," she said to herself. "We all are until Anthony is dealt with," she added, further creeping herself out.

Tia finished her meal, placed the glass in the sink, and made her way back to the bedroom. She climbed into the middle of the bed and wrapped her arms around her drawn up knees while she listened for any movement in the dark. When she was certain nothing was moving outside but a light breeze, she relaxed and stretched out on the bed.

✝

Marcus sat concealed in the darkness of Kaitlin's back stoop, across from Devin and Tia's home, listening to the slowing of her heartbeat while Tia began to drift off to sleep. He worried that someone so important to their success was left unguarded and picked up his phone to make a call. He would wait until one of the strongest of his clan arrived to watch over her until her wolf returned to protect her. Then he would make sure she was protected every night until their plan was complete. He tucked his phone into his jacket and whispered on the breeze, "Sweet dreams, our little spell binder."

✝

Just after midnight, a side door opened and a large man stepped out of the house. He was alone and took no caution in stepping out into the night. He walked to the front sidewalk and, for a second, hesitated and looked in the direction of where Alix was hiding.

A loud noise in the alley made his hackles rise and Devin could sense he was close to shifting when a large raccoon waddled out of the darkness after raiding a nearby garbage can. He snarled at the animal and watched it disappear, his wolf on edge and ready to jump into the fray while his eyes scanned the alley.

Her heart threatened to race out of her chest for several long seconds until the man turned his attention back to the south and resumed walking. Devin waited several seconds to ensure no others would follow him outside, and then she turned and began tracking him while he strolled confidently down the sidewalk, leaving Win alone in the shadows.

✝

Devin followed the man through the darkness, using the shadows from clouds crossing the moon to conceal her from curious eyes. He walked within a half block of the location where they had the SUV concealed, but there was no indication he had picked up any of their scents. When he arrived at his chosen location, a small neighborhood grocery, Devin sat in the shadows of a front stoop to wait for him. When he emerged carrying several bags and walked back in the direction of the townhouse, she assumed he had been sent for food for the three Weres. She followed from a distance until she was sure that he was returning home then turned left and trotted easily back to the club.

She sat under a large tree at the end of the parking lot and waited for the others to arrive. Better planning would have been to stash a set of clothes for her at the club and she could have at least waited inside for her companions.

Fortunately, her wait was not a long one. Alix and Win pulled into the parking lot and Devin shifted and returned to the vehicle to dress. "Was there any other movement after I left?" she asked.

"Nothing outside and it was difficult to detect much movement inside. I caught a quick glimpse of another man when the first one returned with bags and slipped inside the side door," Win answered.

"He was on a grocery run," Devin answered. "Did you have any better luck from your location?" she asked Alix.

"I didn't see any others, but we were right about there being vamp and Were scent. That's definitely Anthony's lair."

"Too bad we couldn't just rush in and stake the bastard," Win surprised them by saying. "The location of his lair makes it impossible for us to ambush him at home."

"Is someone getting impatient?" Alix teased her.

Win looked at her lover. "I'm just ready for this job to be done so we can have some fun." Devin looked at Alix and knew that Alix didn't buy the story any more than she did. Win was a hunter. One who was ready to hunt.

"What's our plan for tomorrow?" Devin asked.

"We'll give Lord Jordan a call in the morning and set up a meeting with Simon to discuss his offer. I'll give you a call or text before noon so you can contact Simon," Win answered.

"I'll wait for your call then," Devin replied and moved to exit the vehicle.

"Do you want me to drop you off?" Alix asked.

"No, it's not far and I could use a walk to clear my head."

"We'll see you tomorrow then," Alix said.

"Goodnight," Devin replied. She stepped from the vehicle and watched them drive away.

She was tempted to step inside the club to check on Kaitlin and Lucia, but worried it would be difficult to fend off the questions Kaitlin would have. Instead, she began walking home and her keen nose picked up the scent of vampire. The closer she came, the stronger the scent became, and she moved faster, until she was running for home. Her body shifted in flight, shredding her clothing and her wolf pounded the street while she ran. When she reached their block, Devin skidded to a halt, her eyes surveying the property until she saw Marcus sitting on the back stoop of Kaitlin's home. Her wolf shifted back to human form.

"What are you doing here?"

"Something you should be doing," he growled. "I'm protecting your spell binder."

Devin chuckled nervously. "You think Tia needs protecting?"

Marcus turned to face her with his cold blue eyes. "Until this ugliness is over, she is the most important asset to our clan and, if I need to remind you, to the success of your mission. Without her aid, you will be defeated."

His words stung Devin's pride, but at some level, she knew he was correct. They would be lost without her magic. "I thank you for the protection," she humbly replied. "I don't know how much longer we will have to be away at night."

"We will be here until this is over," Marcus assured her.

"Thank you," she said, and walked to her home.

†

Devin locked the door behind her before she stepped into the darkened apartment. She could hear Tia's slow heartbeat from the bedroom and knew her lover was sleeping soundly. Devin walked into the kitchen to find a small plate and glass in the sink and decided she would have a sandwich before she laid down to rest. She opened the refrigerator and took out ham, cheese, and mayonnaise to make a sandwich, and the ever-present pitcher of tea to pour a glass. She made a thick sandwich and was standing at the counter eating it while she gazed across the yard. Her eyesight picked up the red tip of a burning cigarette, and she knew Marcus or one of his clan was still present watching over them. Devin decided she would not tell Tia about their presence for fear of making her more anxious. Deep down it was comforting to know that someone was watching over Tia while she was away, even if it was a vampire.

Devin finished off the sandwich and tea, placed her glass next to the one Tia had left, and walked into the bedroom. The blinds were slightly open and the moonlight falling across Tia's face made her more beautiful than ever. Her dark hair fanned over her pillow and a smile formed on her lips. Devin crept between the cool covers, surrounding Tia's body with her larger form.

"I was beginning to wonder if you were coming home tonight," Tia whispered when Devin's warm body snuggled in next to her.

"I could hardly wait to get here," Devin answered. Her hand found Tia's naked stomach and she began to caress her soft skin. "Did you have a good day?"

Devin's touch left a river of desire burning deep within Tia, and it took great restraint to focus on an answer to the question. "Marie worked me like a dog today and has me drinking the most god-awful tea for energy."

Devin chuckled. "I know exactly what you're talking about. Miss Anna had me drink some of it after we dealt with Cedra to help me regain my strength faster. It is wicked stuff but the results are amazing."

"Did you all have a productive day?"

"Yes, we did. We've found Anthony's lair."

"Where is he?"

"Only about ten blocks from here on Esplanade."

Tia rolled over onto her side facing her. "That's very close," she replied with a frown.

"Too close for my comfort," Devin answered.

Tia let her hand run down Devin's side. "I felt like someone was watching me earlier tonight. You don't think he knows we're on to him do you?"

Devin remained silent for a few seconds. So much for

keeping Lord Jordan's protection detail a secret from her, she thought, but better for her to know it was not Anthony hunting her. "You were being watched tonight and still are," she replied.

"What?" Tia cried out sitting up in bed.

"Lord Jordan has decided you need his protection until this mess is over. When I came home, Marcus was here, and he told me they'll be watching over you, especially when I am not around."

"Do they think I am that defenseless?" Tia huffed.

"No, my love, they know you are that important. Without you we're lost," Devin reminded her, and pulled her back down on the bed for a soft kiss.

Tia's lips parted instinctively to invite Devin inside for a deeper kiss.

Devin kissed her with such passion it left no doubt for Tia how much Devin had missed her. She rolled on top of Tia and her body rocked gently between Tia's legs. Their hearts beat with one racing rhythm when they made love, peaking together, and then remaining entwined while they made slow, tender love until they were both consumed by exhaustion. Tia tucked herself into Devin's protective arms and slept peacefully while Devin caressed her back and reviewed the day's events.

In the silence of their bedroom, Devin finally realized how critical Tia's role had become, and she worried for their safety for the first time since they met. She wondered if she would be strong enough to protect Tia during the conflict with Anthony. She would have to be, she finally told herself. Not only their love, but also their lives depended on keeping Tia safe while she worked her magic.

Chapter Nine

Devin woke with a start to find she was alone in bed. Her sleep, filled with dreams, had brought her little rest. She wiped a weary hand over her eyes and climbed from the bed in search of Tia. She took a robe hanging by the door to cover her nakedness while she walked through the house. There was no sign of Tia, but the coffee pot was full and a note sat on the counter beside her favorite mug.

The note read: *Gone to get an early start with Marie. Call me later. Last night was fantastic. Love you. Tia*

Devin smiled, poured a mug of coffee, and took Tia's note to the kitchen table with her. The sun was pouring through the windows with a promise of another beautiful muggy day in New Orleans. She checked the time and then decided on some breakfast and a hot shower before calling Win.

†

"I swear to whatever God will listen that you are trying to kill me," Tia complained to Marie when she downed the first dose of the awful green tea.

Marie chuckled then she bit into a beignet, the powdered sugar falling onto her ample bosom while she watched the faces Tia was making. "Tell me you don't feel stronger, and I won't make you drink another sip," she challenged.

"I can't, this stuff does seem to be working, but—damn—why does it have to taste so bad?"

Marie passed her the mint to chew and then pushed a beignet in front of her. "Eat," she instructed. "You need all the energy you can muster because today you are casting the spell."

Tia chewed the mint before she reached for the tasty treat. "Do you think I'm ready?"

"To be successful, maybe not, but we won't know until you try." Marie took another bite, and when she finished chewing she asked, "Did you practice last night?"

Tia wiped the sugar from her lips with the tip of her tongue. "For several hours, until I was exhausted."

Marie smiled brightly at her. "It needs to be familiar to you like your own name, so we will practice until you are ready to try it on a living being."

Tia nearly dropped the pastry. "You want me to cast it on you?"

"Heavens no, even I'm not that crazy."

Tia cocked her head to the side. "Who then?" she asked.

Marie grinned and called, "Rue Paul, come here boy."

Tia burst out laughing when the innocent little Chihuahua pranced into the kitchen, his tiny claws making tapping sounds on the tile floor. "Isn't that animal cruelty?"

Marie reached down and swooped up the tiny dog into her arms. "There is no way I would let you harm one hair on my precious little boy's head."

"Oh, no pressure there at all," Tia groaned.

"Quit being a worrywart and finish your breakfast. We have a lot to accomplish today. First Rue Paul, and then we move on to Marcus."

Tia nearly choked when she heard that news. "Has anyone told Marcus yet?"

"Not yet, but he would be the closest in age and strength to Anthony, so he would be a great test subject."

"I'm not sure if I'm ready for that," Tia replied, feeling a total lack of confidence.

Marie reached over and patted her arm. "Relax, you're a natural, and you will be ready today. I plan to work you very hard."

Tia soon found out Marie was not kidding. She eventually began to feel sorry for Rue Paul when Marie took him into the living room and then called him into the kitchen repeatedly until Tia could stop him in his tracks when he reached the tile floor. The poor dog stood there whimpering each time she froze him, unable to run to his mistress for protection.

When they took a short break, Tia picked him up in her arms and stroked him gently. She could feel him trembling under her touch. "I am so sorry if I'm scaring you," she cooed to him softly.

"He's no worse for wear," Marie stated. "I will prepare him a special treat tonight as a reward for being such a good puppy."

Tia's phone rang.

"Here let me take him," Marie said, and Tia reached

for her phone.

"Hey, sweetheart," Devin greeted when Tia answered the phone. "How's your day going?"

"Pretty good so far. I'm able to stop a three-pound Chihuahua in his tracks," she stated proudly.

"That's a very good start," Devin agreed, working hard to stifle a chuckle.

"What are you doing?"

"I'm waiting for Win and Alix. We're going to the levee to spar. Then we'll set up a meeting with Lord Jordan to discuss some plans. Will six be fine with you?"

"Hang on just a second," Tia said, and she turned to Marie. "What time do you want to go see Marcus?"

"We'll call him after lunch and request to meet with him at six. I would think a couple of hours would wear you out."

Tia turned her attention back to the phone call. "Six will be fine. Marie and I will meet you there."

"Meet us there?" Devin asked.

"That's right. Marie has this insane idea I should practice on Marcus now that I have Rue Paul under my complete control." Tia suppressed a laugh.

"No time like the present. We'll see you there then. I love you."

"Love you too. Be safe and don't let the kitty cat hurt you too bad."

Devin let out a soft growl at her lover's taunt. "I will try my best."

"See you soon. Bye."

Tia was chuckling when she ended the call. Marie looked at her with a cocked eyebrow. "Are you ready to get serious again?" she asked.

"Yes, ma'am. Do you think Rue Paul is ready?"

†

Alix followed Devin's bike while they made their way to the levee and parked deep in the dense woods. They left the vehicles behind and walked down to a clearing Devin felt would be isolated enough to be safe from prying eyes. When they reached the clearing, Win suggested they sit and talk over strategy for a few moments.

Devin found a shady spot under a large oak and they sat on the ground. "What do you expect the encounter to be like?" Devin asked.

"I would presume that Anthony will spread his three rogues out to either side of him, or maybe even have one behind him to guard his back," Win suggested. "I will need to be on Tia's right side to be most effective in dealing with Anthony, and I would suggest you be on her left. Alix will be to my right."

"What if all three are on one side of Anthony," Alix asked.

"Then you and Devin would both be on that side. I would suggest that if you are forced to fight side by side that Devin is always the one closer to Tia in case she gets in trouble."

"What kind of jeopardy do you think she will be in?" Devin asked.

Win smiled at her before speaking. "Anthony is very strong, and will attempt to make eye contact with Tia quickly when he realizes what she is, and he will try to control or read her thoughts. Marie will probably anticipate this and train Tia how to block him from her mind. She has to fully concentrate on weaving the spell for it to be successful." She cleared her throat and continued. "We cannot allow Tia to become distracted or Anthony to approach too closely. None of us can defeat him if he is at full speed within ten feet of us."

She pulled her revolver from the holster sewed into her cargo pants and opened the cylinder, removing one of the bolts. She lifted it so Devin could get a closer look. "These are made especially for Weres. The last four inches, dipped in pure silver, will cause significant pain for any Were. I plan to release my full load of six bolts in the direction of Anthony and his mutts when we begin, and if we're lucky I may be able to eliminate one of the Weres altogether. I doubt I will hit Anthony, but if I can sink a few into his companions, it should distract them very painfully," she explained with a wicked grin. "Hopefully their cries of pain, will take his attention away from Tia for a few seconds."

Devin eyed the bolt closely. "What kind of affect would it have on Anthony?"

Win looked at her directly. "Unless I found his heart, there would be very little damage to him. They have also been soaked in Holy water, but I doubt that would affect him much at his age."

Devin let her words sink in for several seconds. "Alix and I will be in Were form, so your shooting will be our cue to attack?"

"That's correct. I hope we can stay in a close formation that will prevent them from spreading out too far. The closer they are together, the better my chances are of hitting one or more of them."

"So you let loose with the bolts and we attack, then what will you do?"

"I'll do this," Win said while she reached behind her neck and drew her sword. "It's made of the finest silver, and will cut through living or dead flesh like butter, but I have to be close to use it."

Devin recognized the danger for the hunter, and realized what would happen if Tia failed to work the spell on Anthony. "So if the spell doesn't work or work fast enough, you're first in the line of attack?"

Win nodded her head. "That's correct. Then you and Alix would be easy targets for Anthony."

"This seems like more of a nightmare every time I think of it," Devin groaned.

Alix spoke her first words since the discussion had started. "Have no doubt my friend, we can and will succeed, but our timing has to be precise."

Devin took her words seriously. "How much experience do you have with wolves?"

"Some, but not as much as I'd like, why?" she asked.

"I was thinking it might be good to save our energy and ask Simon to bring three of his best for us to practice on tonight when we meet. Tia will be there this afternoon to practice the spell on Marcus, so we could practice different scenarios with live attackers."

Devin saw the sparkle in Alix's eyes. "That is an excellent idea. Call him and set it up and then we can go for a nice lunch."

Win looked at her lover. "Are you starving again already? It hasn't been long since you had breakfast."

"Not starving, but I can always eat," Alix replied with a wink to Devin. "I could go for some more fried chicken and Mama's macaroni and cheese."

"Mama's has great ribs too," Devin told her.

"Even better," Alix purred.

"Okay, so you call Simon, and set up a meet for late

afternoon. I'll call Lord Jordan to let him know of our plan so he doesn't worry when all of the Weres converge on his lair."

Alix jumped to her feet and offered a hand up to Win. Devin pulled out her cell phone, and walked out into the clearing to make her call to Simon while Win called Lord Jordan.

✝

"Again, and even faster this time," Marie yelled at Tia, before calling Rue Paul to her.

The little dog froze in place when he lifted a paw to step on the tile floor, and Tia smiled. The spell was coming to her much easier and faster. She was pleased with the progress she had made during the morning.

"Okay, that's good," Marie said. Tia released the spell from the dog who took off down the hall.

"That was much easier than the first few attempts this morning," she said with a grin.

"Yes, but that was on Rue Paul. He wasn't trying to read your thoughts, he was just coming for attention and a treat. Your true test will begin with Marcus."

The look of concern on Marie's face deflated the confidence Tia was feeling.

"Come on let's get you a cup of tea and then you can treat me to Mama's fried chicken for lunch."

Tia chuckled. "You do realize you will have to ride on the back of my bike, yes?"

"I have been on a motorcycle or two in my time. There's not as much hair for the breeze to blow through, but I do enjoy a thrilling ride."

"That my dear, you shall have, I promise," Tia replied with a grin. "I'm afraid you'll have to wear a helmet though."

"No worries." Marie grinned when she pushed the hair back from her face.

†

They were on their second round of food when Devin looked up to see Tia and Marie pulling up on her bike. "Would you look at that?"

Alix and Win turned toward the window and spotted what Devin was seeing. Tia had dismounted, and shook her hair free of the helmet while Marie struggled to toss her leg over the seat to make a less than graceful move to get off the bike. Tia smiled and offered her hand to Marie to keep her from stumbling when the toe of her shoe caught the low bike seat.

Devin stood and walked to the front door to help them inside. When she opened the door and Tia saw her, she smiled warmly. "Imagine meeting you here. Is there any food left?"

She smiled back at her lover. "I bet Mama could round up a bologna sandwich or something," she teased. "Hey, Marie," she said and leaned down to kiss her cheek. "Has my girl been behaving herself today?"

Marie smiled up at her. "Yes she's been very good, but I worry poor Rue Paul may never be the same."

"Come join us," Devin requested. She led them to the table and motioned for a server.

"Alix, Win, this is Miss Marie." Tia made the introductions.

133

Marie looked at them, then at the food on the table and shook her head. "Someone has worked up a good appetite."

"You know that doesn't take much for us," Devin reminded her.

The sassy server walked up to the table with her order pad in hand. "I hope you two don't want chicken, I think these three have eaten the last dozen chickens we had," she teased with a wink to Alix.

"Actually I did have my heart set on some of Mama's chicken," Marie said, thinking the server serious.

"For you, I will go chase a few birds down myself," she told Marie.

"Excellent, some macaroni and cheese and beans too?" she asked.

"That does sound good. Make it two please," Tia requested.

"Sweet tea?" the server asked.

"Nothing better," Tia answered.

"Coming right up then." The server walked back toward the kitchen.

Devin watched her leave and turned to Tia. "There's been a change in plans."

"Anthony has gone elsewhere?" she asked, teasing.

"If only. No, we are going to Lord Jordan's with you. We have invited Simon and three of his best to run through some combat scenarios so we can see what we will be dealing with while you test your new skills on Marcus."

"Oh sheesh, I have to do it in front of an audience?"

"Don't worry, you're ready," Marie assured her, patting her arm.

Tia looked at her with a bashful smile. "I'm glad you're feeling confident."

"Just have some faith in your skills," Marie told her.

"We'll have our hands too full to be a distraction to you," Alix promised.

Devin looked at Win. "Do you have rubber bolts that you can use in your revolver?"

Win looked at her and grinned. "Sort of," she stated. "I use a paintball gun of the same dimensions as my revolver, with bright pink balls, so I can see where my shots have landed. I hope Simon and his pack don't mind pink."

"If your shots hit their mark, I don't think they'll mind about the color," Devin assured her. "Maybe a bit of damaged pride, but they will realize the importance of their roles in this process."

When their meals were finished, they decided to return to their homes for a brief rest before meeting up at Lord Jordan's later in the day. Marie accepted a ride from Alix and Win, who would retrieve her later for the ride to Lord Jordan's home.

Devin and Tia watched them depart, and then Devin turned to her lover. "I think it is time we talk with Kaitlin."

Tia drew in a deep breath. "I know you're right, but I don't know how well she's going to take the news."

"I know of only one way to find out," Devin replied as she pulled her helmet on. "Let's go get this over with."

Tia nodded and mounted her bike to follow Devin home.

Chapter Ten

Devin and Tia parked their bikes just outside of the garage. They would be leaving again in a couple hours and there was no threat of rain. Devin walked over to Tia, and took her hand when they began to walk toward Kaitlin's home.

"Are you ready for this?"

"No, but I agree Kaitlin needs to know what is going on. I can't bear the thought of lying to her. She has been too good to me to be treated like that."

"I understand, and agree completely," Devin told her.

†

Lucia was having lunch with Kaitlin when they heard the rumble of the approaching bikes. Kaitlin looked up when Devin and Tia arrived and parked by the garage.

"I wonder what those two are up to now," she said to Lucia.

"I have no idea, but it looks like we are about to find

out," Lucia answered when Tia and Devin stepped onto the porch.

"Come on in," Kaitlin hollered, when Devin lifted her hand to knock.

Devin took a deep breath and opened the door, holding it to allow Tia to step through first.

"Hey, ladies," Kaitlin said.

"Hi, Kaitlin, and you too, Lucia." Tia slipped in beside Kaitlin.

"Have you two had lunch?" she asked.

"Yes thanks, Kaitlin," Devin answered. "Do you have some time to talk?" She took a seat next to Lucia.

"Yes I do," Kaitlin answered, a worried frown on her face.

"I guess that's my cue to move on," Lucia replied, and started to stand.

Devin moved her hand to Lucia's arm. "You might as well stay."

Lucia looked at her friend and nodded.

"It's time for us to be honest with Kaitlin."

"Honest about what?" Kaitlin asked with a tremble in her voice.

"Of who, and what we are," Devin replied. "You deserve to know what we're involved in."

Tia wriggled under Kaitlin's gaze. "I think we all need a drink," she said, and grabbed a bottle of Jack and four glasses to bring to the table.

Devin watched her pour and then began speaking to Kaitlin. "What we are going to tell you may be very shocking to you, but I think I can speak for all three of us when I tell you we love you and appreciate all you have done for us."

Kaitlin's hand went to her chest. "You all should know I love you too, but you're beginning to scare me, Devin. Is there something wrong?"

"Yes, something is very wrong, but I must tell you other things first. You need to know who and what we are."

"Are you secret government agents or something?" Kaitlin guessed.

Devin couldn't resist a chuckle. "No, we aren't spooks." She reached across the table to place a comforting hand on Kaitlin's arm. "Do you believe in supernatural beings?"

"Like ghosts or the devil?" Kaitlin asked.

"No, more like witches, vampires, and werewolves," Devin answered.

Kaitlin's face drained of color when Devin's words sank in to her consciousness. "This is New Orleans, and it does have a history of voodoo and witchery." She attempted to be lighthearted.

"But, do you believe?"

"Honestly, I have never given it much thought. What are you trying to tell me?"

Devin took a deep breath and let it out slowly. "Lucia and I are werewolves, and Tia is a spell binder, or what you might call a witch."

Kaitlin chuckled while the three friends watched her closely. "You're kidding me right?"

"No, Kaitlin, I am very serious," Devin, answered, while Tia placed an arm around Kaitlin's shoulders.

"I've just recently learned about my powers, but Devin and Lucia were born werewolves," Tia explained.

Kaitlin picked up the glass in front of her with the strong whiskey and downed it, bringing the color back to her face.

They watched while the realization of what Devin and Tia were saying washed over Kaitlin. "A-a-a witch and werewolves, you say?" she stammered.

"Yes," Devin answered, slowly nodding her head. "Tia, I think it would be less terrifying if you were to demonstrate rather than me or Lucia," she told her lover.

Tia responded by holding her fisted hand across the middle of the table, and when she opened her hand, a ball of flames danced on her palm.

Kaitlin's eyes grew wide for several long seconds, and her friends were worried she would faint. Tia quickly closed her palm, extinguishing the flame.

"Holy shit," Kaitlin cried, staring at Tia.

"I know this is difficult news for you to receive, but something very dangerous is going on, and we felt you needed to be aware of what's about to happen. To do that we have to disclose this information to you with the faith that you can accept it, can protect our identity and our trust in you," Devin stated.

Kaitlin nodded her understanding, unable to form words to speak.

"New Orleans has a very strong presence of vampires," Devin stated, and winced at the fear crossing Kaitlin's face. "They are no threat to the human population here, but they are under attack by someone who would be a serious threat to humans, and other supernatural beings, like us," Devin continued.

"So how does that involve you two?"

"Alix and Win are bounty hunters who handle situations like these, and they are under contract with the leader of the New Orleans vampires. Unfortunately, the vampire they are hunting is too strong for them to handle alone, and there are three rogue werewolves accompanying him. Because of our skills and experiences, we've been asked to help. The werewolves that accompany him will be an issue for my pack in Baton Rouge if we fail, and I cannot let that happen."

"Wow," Kaitlin stated.

"I know that this is a lot of information at one time, but we had to share it with you."

Kaitlin's eyes grew wide. "Am I in danger?"

Devin smiled at her. "No, our prey does not know who we are or what we are planning." Devin hesitated for a second. "I have asked Lucia to watch over you and there is extra protection here at night, just as a precaution."

Kaitlin's eyes darted over to look at Lucia, who smiled at her.

"What is going to happen?"

"We've been training to be prepared to confront the enemy," Tia replied. "Over the next few nights we hope to encounter and defeat them."

Kaitlin reached for the bottle and poured another strong drink. "That sounds very dangerous to you. Is there not any other way?" Kaitlin asked with genuine concern.

"No, we've run out of options," Devin answered.

Kaitlin heard the sadness and worry in Devin's voice when she spoke, and took a long drink.

"Is there anything I can do to help?"

"Pray for us if you believe in a higher power," Devin answered. "We need all the help we can get."

"Oh dear," Kaitlin cried, again clutching her chest in worry.

"We have to succeed, Kaitlin, or everything changes for the worse for New Orleans, and for my pack," Devin said.

They watched Kaitlin while their words began to sink in.

"I know that you're risking everything by telling me this. I would never dream of doing anything to hurt any of you," Kaitlin said.

"You are family to us," Tia stated. "We had to tell you this."

"Thank you," Kaitlin replied. She took Tia's glass of whiskey and finished it.

"Are you going to be okay?" Devin asked her.

"I'll be fine, it's you all that I am afraid for," she answered.

"Have some faith in us," Tia replied with a wink. "We're a pretty bad ass team."

"Are Win and Alix like you?"

"Win is completely human but an exceptional hunter and fighter. Alix is a werecat, and when she shifts, she transforms into a large black panther."

"Oh my," Kaitlin replied, clearly suffering from information overload.

"Thank you for being so supportive to all of us," Devin told her. "We have a full evening of training planned, so if you will excuse us, Tia and I need some rest."

Kaitlin jumped from her seat, and hugged Tia and then Devin. "Please be careful," she said.

"We will," Devin assured her. "I have no plans of letting anything happen to either of us."

Lucia also stood to leave. "Let me know when you're ready to go to the club."

"I will, and thanks for all you are doing, too," Kaitlin replied.

They left the house together and Lucia looked at

Devin. "I thought that went well."

"Better than we anticipated. I hope you didn't mind me outing you."

Lucia chuckled. "Kaitlin would have asked if you didn't. She's a sharp one."

"That she is," Devin agreed. "We may see you later," she added and then she and Tia walked to their home.

They walked straight into the bedroom and undressed to climb into bed. "I've set the alarm for five," Devin stated then she turned to take Tia in her arms.

"I love you," Tia said and kissed her.

"I love you too," Devin answered when Tia snuggled into her body.

†

Across town, Win snuggled into Alix. Alix held her close while Win slept, but rest would not come for her. Her mind could not shut down while she worried about the impending encounter. Had they bitten off more than they could chew in this endeavor? Should they just swallow their pride and go home, forfeiting the handsome contract? These and other questions swarmed in her mind while she tried not to toss and turn to wake Win. Alix knew the answers even though the questions kept pouring into her brain. They had to finish this contract. It was who they were, and dangerous as it might be, this was when they shone their brightest.

Alix sighed and placed a forearm across her eyes, willing her brain to turn off so she could rest.

†

Lord Jordan stretched out on the sofa while Marcus prepared them a drink. "So how do you feel about being the spell binder's test subject?" he asked him.

Marcus looked up from pouring their drinks. "I will do whatever's necessary for them to be successful. I just hope she knows the spell, and doesn't turn me into a toad or something else hideous."

"That's the spirit," Lord Jordan replied with a chuckle. "I don't believe Marie would be suggesting the tests if Tia wasn't ready. I think it was an excellent idea to ask Simon and a few of his pack to participate to give them an opportunity to work through the scenarios of real combat with live enemies."

"I agree, it needs to be as realistic as possible," Marcus added. He picked up the glasses and carried them into the room. He handed one to Lord Jordan. "What do you believe their chances of survival are?"

"That all depends on Tia and how well she performs. I have every confidence in Alix, Win, and Devin taking on the werewolves, but Anthony can be devious. He will not hesitate to sacrifice his companions to ensure his own safety. He will be focused on only one thing once he realizes who Tia is, to possess her for her skills." He took a sip of the rich red liquid and sighed. "That would never happen while Devin is alive, but that does give me pause to worry."

"Are the two Weres strong enough to defeat three?" Marcus asked.

Lord Jordan chuckled at his question. "I have seen footage of Win's abilities. I think by the time she lets fly her round of bolts, the score will be more even. Harley trained her well and she can shoot with either hand with deadly efficiency."

"What about her skills with the sword?" Marcus questioned.

A gleam of excitement flashed in his eyes. "She's even better than Harley, much faster than he even dreamed."

"Do you plan to be present when the confrontation occurs?"

"You and I will be concealed close by, but we cannot intervene unless they are defeated."

"Let's hope it doesn't come to that," Marcus replied. "I would hate to have to explain to Damien Benoit why his only sister was killed."

"Devin is doing what is honorable for her clan," Lord Jordan reminded him.

"Honorable or not, I don't relish the thought of his rage."

"Work them hard tonight then, and do everything you can to prepare them."

Marcus nodded his head in understanding. "If you will excuse me then, I will go change clothes and prepare."

†

"Will you join us for dinner when we finish tonight?" Win asked Marie after she climbed into the back seat.

"Yes, that would be lovely," Marie, answered. "May I suggest Crescent City? I believe you will find it much to your liking."

"We will drop you home and then shower and change clothes before returning for you," Alix said.

"I'll call and make a reservation for us. Will ten thirty be good?"

Alix smiled back at her. "We'll be starving by then, but that will be fine."

"Trust me, it will be worth your wait," Marie promised.

✝

When they arrived at Lord Jordan's estate, Tia and Devin were already there and had parked their bikes. They were talking with Simon and three of the largest men Win had ever seen. "My goodness they're big," she said when they pulled up.

"The bigger they are, the harder they fall, or at least I hope," Alix said from the passenger seat.

"Courage, ladies, you will be fine," Marie reassured them.

"Let's get this party started then. I hope to have a huge steak waiting for me," Alix replied to shift the mood.

✝

The sun was rapidly fading when the large group approached the front door. Marcus met them at the door, his eyes wide with surprise at the size of the men Simon had brought with him.

"Please come in," he requested, holding the door wide. "We will be practicing in the courtyard."

They walked down a long hallway through the house.

"Simon, Lord Jordan has asked that you join him in the parlor to watch the activities on video," Marcus instructed, and pointed to the parlor doors.

Simon stopped and turned to Devin. "I will come out

145

and let you know if I can share some tips after watching a few bouts. Take it easy on my guys." He winked and left to join Lord Jordan.

"We will," she answered with a grin. Devin noticed that Marcus was dressed in much more casual clothes than she had ever seen, and she was pleased he was taking his role in this practice seriously.

Marcus opened a door and they emerged into a large, grassy courtyard, which would provide ample room to complete their maneuvers.

"This is an excellent spot," Win said.

Marcus nodded. "What are your plans for us?"

Win took the lead just like everyone had expected. "We want to create a variety of scenarios that we may face during our confrontation with Anthony. We know he has three rogues, but we need to practice a variety of alignments."

Marie stepped closer to Marcus. "You will be the center point of activity. Hold no punches while you approach Tia, and think of every trick Anthony may throw at her," she explained.

Win pulled out her gun and held it out for all to see. She looked at the three Weres and then Marcus. "I need to be as realistic as possible to practice my aim, but these are only paintballs, and I promise they will wash off easily, but they will sting a bit."

"Very well," Jonah, the largest of Simon's men replied. "Are we ready to proceed?"

"Yes," Win answered. "Remember, no claws, and no teeth. We don't need anyone injured tonight."

Jonah nodded, and the five Weres began the process of shifting.

Marie pulled Tia off to the side. "Remember to block

Marcus from entering your mind, and weave the spell as fast as you can."

Tia wiped her sweating hands on her jeans. She was anxious and her body was reacting to her emotions. She hoped after tonight's exercises that she would feel more confident and less anxious about her abilities.

When it appeared everyone was ready, Win spoke to Marcus and the three Weres. "Move back twenty-five feet. I want one Were to the right of Marcus, and two to the left."

Tia stood with Devin on her left and Win on her right. Alix was to Win's right and faced the two wolves while they turned. She could feel Marcus staring at her, trying to enter her mind. She smiled at him when they locked eyes, and she used her training to block him. If she could keep his, and then Anthony's eyes locked with hers, then they would concentrate only on her, and not her companions.

When Marie said, "Begin," everyone began to move forward.

Instinctively, the wolves fanned out to make room for combat, and Win knew she would have to unload her gun quickly before her odds of hitting them diminished. She was the first to react to movement, and she lifted her gun, spraying a round of six paintballs into the approaching force.

Marcus picked up speed and Tia realized too late how fast he was when she began weaving her spell. By the time he had closed to within ten feet, she had barely slowed his movement. Her body trembled with fear when she realized she had failed the first attempt.

†

Win heard a sharp yip from one of the wolves and,

playing his part, he went down to the ground. Her paintball had hit him directly over his heart, a killing blow for any supernatural creature. He was the second wolf from the right. Her first shot had been high and missed the wolf completely. She smiled when she saw a bright pink dot on Marcus' right side, but she knew it would only slow him slightly. She looked further down the line to the final wolf, the one facing Devin and saw a pink dot above his hindquarter. That would be a great shot with a bolt, not totally disabling him, but sending enough pain through his body to throw him off stride and distract him. She dropped her gun and reached for her sword, only to realize she would be too late. Marcus was barely an arm's length away from her, and would be on her before she could swing. It was another two paces before Marcus felt his muscles freeze as the spell took control of him. A glance at Devin and Alix found them grappling with the two wolves. It would be difficult to gauge how they would perform without going into full combat mode and that was too dangerous for them at this point of the game.

"Stop," Marie called. "Tia, you just got everyone killed," she chastised her sharply. "You must be faster."

Tia's head drooped and she doubted her speed.

"You can do this, just be faster in beginning your spell," Marcus surprised her by speaking. "You blocked me well, but the spell was too slow."

Tia took encouragement from his unexpected comments. "I can do this," she said aloud to herself.

Win replaced the sword in its sheath and picked up the gun to begin reloading. "Everyone okay?" she asked, looking primarily to the wolves who nodded, unable to speak in wolf form. "Let's do it again, same formation."

Marie stepped to Tia's side. "Put less emphasis on blocking Marcus this time, and more on the spell. Let's see if he can block you from the spell."

"So don't try to block him at all?" Tia asked for clarification.

"Only if you feel he can prevent you from casting the spell," Marie answered.

†

Simon entered the parlor, and took a seat while Lord Jordan poured them each a large glass of bourbon. A large video screen was lowered for viewing, and they watched while the group prepared for the training.

"Has Win shared with you Devin's plan for my pack to assist in securing two of the properties in the hope of driving Anthony to Canal Street?"

"Yes, I think that's a solid plan. Will you also be close by in case their efforts fail?" Lord Jordan asked.

"I will have six of my best in position to initiate a strike within seconds if they fail," Simon promised. "I pray it doesn't come to that."

"I'll also have a group in place if we need to step in and finish the job," Lord Jordan replied.

They sipped the bourbon and watched while the action on the screen moved forward.

"Not bad for a first attempt," Simon said to him, when the first round ended.

"Agreed. Let's just hope she can pick up speed now that she knows more about who she is facing."

†

It took two more attempts for Tia to determine how

much effort she would need to block Marcus and still be able to weave the spell. Win adjusted her aim and managed to hit all three wolves, effectively removing one each round. One on one, Alix and Devin were able to drive their opponents away from Marcus, becoming less of a distraction to Tia and Win.

On the third attempt, Tia was perfect and froze Marcus three steps into the battle. The spell came to her as easily as breathing now that she had the right cadence. Win dropped one wolf and had her sword within six inches of Marcus' neck within seconds of his freeze.

"Perfect," Marie praised. "Now change alignments."

Two wolves shifted to Devin's side, overloading the left. The alignment proved more difficult for Win, causing her to have to aim well beyond Marcus, but she still inflicted significant damage.

They ran through three more sessions, and Marie could feel Tia's strength draining away.

"I think we've done all we can here without totally exhausting Tia," Marie warned. "Let's move back inside for a cool drink and discuss what we learned."

Win would have loved a few more attempts, but she agreed that they did not want to exhaust Tia. The Weres shifted back into human form and dressed.

"Remind me to never battle you with paint guns," Jonah said to Win. "Your shooting skills are impressive."

"I hope I didn't hurt any of you too bad," she answered with a wink.

"I think we'll live," Jonah replied with a chuckle. "The first one stung like hell though," he added about the shot she had placed over his heart.

"It was much easier when the alignment was overloaded to my right side," she told the group.

"You didn't do horribly on either side," Marcus said as they began walking inside. Marcus looked at Tia with a smile. "I would have never thought you could freeze me like that, but you did."

Tia smiled with his praise, but she was weary. "Thanks, Marcus. Did you hold back at all?"

"Not one bit," he answered. "I gave it every bit of trickery I could, and you were still successful."

"Good," she replied, and took Devin's arm for support.

"Hit him with everything you've got straightaway. You won't have a second chance," Marcus warned.

"I will," Tia replied with a forced smile.

✝

When they saw the group walking toward the house, Simon turned to Lord Jordan. "What do you think?"

"I think she can do it, but it will take all the energy from her," he warned.

"Let's hope that will be enough."

"Come, my friend, you can help me pour drinks." Lord Jordan motioned Simon to the bar.

✝

When the group reached the house Marcus stepped to the side. "Tia, will you and Devin stay with me a second more?"

The others walked into the house, leaving them alone with Marcus.

"I had one more thing I feel I need to share with

151

you," he said.

Tia looked at him with interest. "What is it?"

"There is one more trick Anthony may use that I haven't shared with you. He is a very handsome figure in human form, but when he attacks, he may choose to appear to you like the creature he truly is, to throw you off, and distract you from the spell." He waited until her focus was completely on him.

"Be prepared to face something that looks like this," Marcus warned and his handsome face transformed into a gruesome demon-like face with large teeth and hideous features.

Tia gasped in shock, and her grip grew tighter on Devin's arm. Marcus quickly shifted back to his human appearance. "Don't be surprised if he shifts," he said with a light blush.

Tia had regained her composure, and she looked at Marcus with compassion. "Thank you for sharing that with me. I would have been caught off guard if I wasn't expecting that."

"Good luck," he stated, and pulled the door open for them.

When they entered the room, Marcus retrieved drinks for them while they settled onto a comfortable sofa.

"Great job everyone," Simon praised.

"Did you see anything we need to change?" Win asked him.

"Not that you haven't already adjusted."

"If my calculations are correct, tomorrow may be a night Anthony chooses to attack," Win reported. "Did Simon share with you our plan for a show of force at the two sites to drive him to opt for the Canal Street location?" she asked Lord Jordan.

"Yes, he did. It sounds like a solid plan."

"Can we be ready for action tomorrow night?" she asked the group.

"We will be there," Simon replied.

"Our group will be focused as well," Marcus, answered.

Win looked at Tia. "That only leaves us. Are we ready?"

Tia lifted her chin to look into Win's eyes and confidently stated, "I am ready."

"He has been striking after full dark, correct?" Win asked Marcus.

"Between eight and ten, yes," he answered.

Win drained her glass then looked at Marcus and Simon. "Have your forces ready and in place by seven, and we will be at the Canal location by seven thirty."

"Get some food and rest tonight, ladies," Lord Jordan said, when they stood to leave. "Happy hunting tomorrow night if we do not talk tomorrow."

"Thanks," Win replied and led the small group out to where they had left their bikes and the SUV.

When they reached the bikes, Alix announced, "We have reservations at ten thirty at Crescent City. That will give us enough time to shower and change clothes. Marie, we'll pick you up on our way. Would you two like to ride with us also?" she asked Devin and Tia.

Devin took in Tia's appearance and saw how tired she was. "Yes, I think that would be best. Do you remember how to get to us, Marie?"

"Yes, I won't get us lost," she replied with a grin.

✝

"You okay to ride?" Devin asked Tia.

"Yeah, but let's go straight home," she answered.

They started their bikes and reached home in record time. Devin parked her bike and rushed to lift the garage door for Tia to drive inside, then pushed her own bike in and closed the door.

Inside the house, Tia pulled out a baggie and asked Devin, "Will you boil some water?"

Devin saw the dark tea leaves in the plastic bag. Marie had given Tia tea to drink to help restore her strength.

Devin took the bag from her and pointed to the bedroom. "Go lay down, and I will prepare a mug for you."

"Thanks," Tia replied, managing a weak smile.

Devin looked at the clock in the kitchen to see it was eight. She would get the tea into Tia and put her to bed for an hour and a half to rest, then they could shower together to save time, and get dressed to meet the others. Devin worked on the tea and when she entered the bedroom, Tia was already fast asleep. She hated to wake her but it was important that she drank the tea. Devin sat on the edge of the bed and gently woke Tia. "Drink this quickly and go back to sleep."

She placed the mug into Tia's hand and she drank the contents quickly and for the first time without complaint, registering with Devin just how tired she was. Devin placed the mug on the bedside table and considered canceling dinner to allow her to rest, but remembered Tia also needed a feast of protein to help her regain her energy.

Devin set the alarm, slipped out of her clothes, and wrapped her body protectively around Tia.

Chapter Eleven

After they dropped Marie off at home, Alix turned to Win. "What did you think of tonight?"

"I think we are as prepared as time will allow us to be," she answered.

"Can we do this?"

"Yes, we can and we will," Win promised. She never remembered Alix being so concerned about a contract before which made her worry about what was affecting her lover's confidence. "Are you okay, sweetheart?"

"Yeah, but I have to admit this scares me," Alix replied.

"I would think we were crazy if we weren't scared," Win said and took Alix's hand in hers. "We have to use the fear to fuel us, and not let it drain our energy and confidence." She felt Alix relax a bit. "Remember. We are two pairs, bound by love, blood, and honor. There is no way he can defeat us."

Alix let her words sink in while they drove back to the hotel. When they had parked and gone upstairs to their room, she took Win in her arms. "You're right like usual. Just think, if this is over tomorrow night we could be home by the weekend."

"Do you miss the farm that much?" Win asked as she brushed Alix's hair from her face.

"I need some long, long runs," Alix replied. "My cat needs to be in control for a while."

Win stroked down her long powerful arms. "I can understand that, and you'll have all the running you could wish, and then you come back to me when you're done."

"Wild horses couldn't drag me away from you," Alix teased.

"Do you want to shower or nap first?"

"Let's rest for a short while, and then we can shower."

†

When the alarm sounded, Tia woke up feeling recharged, leaving Devin staring at her, mouth agape when Tia pulled her toward the shower. Less than two hours ago Tia had barely made it to the bed. "Come on, Devin, we need to get a move on, I'm starving."

"Hey, that's usually my line," Devin replied with a chuckle as Tia shucked her clothes and started the shower.

Tia turned back to Devin, her eyes sparkling. "I think I might get a big steak tonight," she said.

Devin smiled to see her so invigorated and hungry, but she knew her idea of a big steak would still be about a third of the size that she herself would be eating. Her chicken feast had long ago burned off and her need for protein growled from deep within her when her wolf reacted to the mention of steak.

She stepped into the shower behind Tia who was already soaking her hair in the warm water.

✝

Marie took Rue Paul out for a break and then fed him a nice dinner. "You have been such a good boy today. Mommy will bring you a nice bone to gnaw on tonight."

Marie knew it was pointless to lie down because easy sleep eluded her these days. Instead, she poured a glass of whiskey and sat in her recliner to enjoy it. Soon she would take a shower. She mentally reviewed the events of the day and was pleased at how well Tia had performed. She sipped the strong drink with a growing confidence that Tia and her friends would succeed in defeating the trespassing vampire. Then, life could return to normal.

Tia would be returning to school in the next few weeks, so her time for studying her craft would be limited primarily to the weekends. Marie would miss her company once she returned to her classes. She understood the importance of Tia to the pack and considered moving back to Baton Rouge to live out her remaining years when they left New Orleans.

"Yes, that would be nice," she spoke aloud to herself. Marie drained her glass and made her way to the bathroom for a shower and change of clothes.

✝

Devin finished dressing and stepped outside into the night. Her senses buzzed and she looked toward the direction of Lucia's apartment while she began to walk. She knew that one of Lord Jordan's clan was there watching and would let him know they would be gone to dinner for several hours so he would not worry. Instead of a male, Devin saw a female, sitting on the stairs, and she approached.

"Are you from Marcus?" she asked.

"Yes, I'm Elana, and I'm assigned to watch over you tonight," the beautiful young vampire said.

"We'll be going out to dinner and will not be back for a while," Devin told her. "So don't worry if it turns into two or three hours, okay?"

The woman gave her a seductive smile. "You must be very hungry," she replied.

"Yes, we are," Devin stated, a little thrown off by the allure of the vamp.

"I'll be here all night, so you can relax, but thank you for letting me know you will be gone for a while."

"You're welcome," Devin answered, and turned to walk back to the house.

"Ms. Benoit," the woman said.

Devin turned back to face her.

"If you ever tire of the witch, look me up," she stated with a chuckle.

Devin smiled. "I'll keep you in mind," she answered and resumed walking.

She was still chuckling to herself when she entered the house.

Tia, waiting for her in the kitchen, asked, "What's so funny?"

"I was just hit on by a female vamp," she answered, still chuckling until she saw Tia's face.

"Where is she? I will turn her into a toad," Tia growled while she stormed toward the door.

"Tia, love, I only have eyes for you," Devin promised and she pulled her lover into her arms for a deep kiss.

Headlights flashing through the darkness alerted them when the SUV pulled onto the property and interrupted their kiss.

"Let's go eat." Devin took Tia's hand when they left the house.

†

"Someone pinch me," Alix said while she reviewed the menu.

Win eagerly reached over and pinched Alix's arm like she had requested, making Alix cry, "Ouch," while the rest cracked up with laughter.

"Damn, I was just teasing," Alix growled, rubbing her arm.

"You need to make that plain next time," Win told her.

Devin had lowered her menu. "You must have spotted the porterhouse for three on the menu."

"Exactly," Alix replied. "I'm glad you understand me."

"What's not to love about three pounds of rare beef?" Devin asked.

"You two are incorrigible," Win groaned. "What are we to do with them?" she asked Tia.

"The only thing we can do, feed them, and keep them happy," Tia replied with a smile.

Marie sat between the two couples, enjoying the friendly banter. The tea's effect on Tia was impressive, and she smiled while the youngsters laughed together, having a good time even with the perils that they faced. Her decision to move back to the compound was looking to be a better decision she thought. She realized how much she missed the energy of youth.

The server returned with their drinks and took their orders with a promise of appetizers and fresh bread to hold them until their meals arrived. Tia was impressed that the woman never batted an eyelash when both Devin and Alix ordered the huge porterhouse steaks.

"She must be familiar with Were appetites," Win whispered to her after the server left.

They feasted on the prime beef, and for several hours did not discuss the dangers they would be facing the following night. Devin laughed, enjoying the company of Alix and Win more than she had ever anticipated.

When the check arrived and Win graciously paid it, a grave cloud came over them. They all knew that this could possibly be the last meal they would share together. None of them wanted to admit it though.

They silently climbed into the vehicle and when they arrived at Devin and Tia's, Marie took Tia's hand.

"Double the amount of tea you drink tomorrow and it wouldn't hurt to share some with Devin," Marie added. "Good luck and I will see you soon."

Tia turned to follow Devin from the vehicle.

"Tia," Marie said. "Remember Ella is with you."

Tia nodded and left the vehicle before her tears could fall. She stood beside Devin and watched the vehicle drive away while she slipped her tiny hand into Devin's large paw.

When the taillights of the SUV disappeared, Devin guided Tia back into their home. She could sense the tingling of the female vamp watching over them and smiled.

Tia heated water for the terrible tea and guzzled it

down, chewing a sprig of mint before racing to the bathroom. Devin let out a soft laugh when she lifted the mug to her lips and drank the tea in one large gulp. She followed Tia into the bathroom to brush her teeth then took her lover to bed.

The flashing of desire in Devin's eyes when they made love always increased Tia's passion and they made love well into the early morning with abandon, each silently fearing this could be their last night on earth together.

✝

Win lay curled up in Alix's arms, listening to the strong heartbeat of her lover. They had faced battle many times together, but never one so important to so many groups; human, vampire and Were. Her fingers traced circles across Alix's taut abdomen, and she could hear the purr from her cat rising from deep inside her body.

Alix lay on her back, her fingers playing in Win's soft hair. Win had become her life after Harley's death, and Alix could not fathom a life without her. She would die protecting her lover, but she could not allow their plan to fail. She did not fear death or the afterworld, but she could not face life without Win by her side. She was her mate for life, and without Win, there would be no point in living. She shivered to shake the somber mood threatening to envelop her completely.

"I know you aren't cold," Win whispered against her skin.

Alix lifted Win's chin to meet her eyes. "I was just thinking about tomorrow."

"It's hard not to think about it, isn't it?" Win asked.

"There's just so much at risk here," Alix answered.

"We won't fail," Win promised while she kissed along Alix's abdomen, following the soft black hairs that lead down her center. She climbed on top of her lover and, for once, Alix allowed her the dominant position.

†

Marie paced her home, the tile clicking loudly under her feet. She struggled with her allegiance to Damien, her Alpha, and her promise to Devin, to not get him involved in the events that were about to unfold in New Orleans. She knew the only way Damien could get involved without breaching Council Mandates would be to avenge his sister's death. Marie knew his wrath would fall upon her shoulders if Devin died in the battle, but she more clearly understood the consequences to the pack if Devin and her friends failed.

Never once in her ninety plus years had she faced such a dilemma. Several times before the sun came up, she had reached for her phone to call Damien, faltering each time while her fingers shook with indecision, and she was unable to dial.

†

The dawn came and brought with it torrential rain that lashed the streets and buildings, keeping everyone but the most desperate inside.

Win crept from the bed and pulled the heavy drapes so they could lie in bed and watch the rain slide down the glass in small rivers. Thunder rumbled in the distance, and lightning flashed across the river.

"I dreamed last night," Alix said when Win snuggled

back into her arms.

Win looked up into her lover's smiling face. "What did you dream?"

"That I was running through the forest at the farm. The cat had ascended and I could smell every creature's scent while I ran down a familiar path. The pine scent was fresh after a morning shower and I could feel every muscle, every tendon, and the blood coursing through my veins while I ran." Alix let her hand stroke Win's velvety skin while she spoke. "I heard the cry of a red-tailed hawk and looked up to see a cloudless blue sky, its color only broken by a jet trail heading north. I felt at peace."

Win felt that was a good omen for them. Alix didn't dream often, but when she did, it had always been a positive sign. "Are you anticipating your first run once we get home?"

"Yes, I am. I'm more than ready to shed the oppressive heat and stench of the city for some clean, fresh air."

"Soon, very soon, my love," Win promised.

Alix's stomach growled.

"Should we order room service?"

Alix chuckled. "Are you afraid of a little rain?"

"No, but if we have room service, I can have you for dessert."

Alix reached over and grabbed the phone off the nightstand. "I'm dialing."

†

Tia woke to the smell of bacon. She stretched, flinging the sheets from around her body and climbed from the bed. She took a robe from the hook, tied it loosely around her, and then she followed her nose to the kitchen. Tia found Devin in front of the stove frying bacon and walked up behind her to wrap her arms around her.

"Good morning," Devin said just as a flash of lightning lit up the room.

"How long has it been raining?"

"About an hour now," Devin answered. "I reckoned if we were going to get breakfast before the power goes out I had better get to cooking." She wrapped an arm around Tia.

"What can I do?"

"Pour me another cup of coffee for starters, and then you can whip up a dozen eggs."

"What are you going to eat?" Tia teased.

Devin grinned. "You did work up an appetite last night."

"What can I say? You are just too irresistible," Tia teased, while her hand moved below Devin's waist.

"Don't forget our tea too," Devin reminded her.

Tia took Devin's mug and refilled it before pouring one of her own. She placed a small pot of water on the stove to boil for their tea and then walked to the refrigerator for the carton of eggs. "What do you want to do today?"

Devin turned the bacon in the pan. "Spend the day in bed relaxing with you," she answered. "We've never done that and I think it's way past time we did."

Tia began cracking eggs into a bowl. "Will you tell me stories of growing up with the pack?"

Devin knew Tia never tired of the stories of adventures she and Damien shared growing up, and she chuckled at the request. "Yes. I will tell you any story you want."

✝

The day passed too quickly for her tastes and at five, Win climbed from the bed to follow Alix into a shower. The rain had finally stopped and the weatherman reported a cold front moving in quickly. They would soon be under a tornado watch while the normal summer temperature, mixed with the moisture of the rain, clashed with the approaching cold front. *A perfect night for a hunt*, she thought with a smile. The weather would keep most everyone inside and away from the potential battlefield.

She stepped into the shower behind Alix and took the soapy cloth from her. She enjoyed the feel of the silky soap while she ran the cloth down her lover's strong back. She could hear the rumbling of her inner cat and turned Alix to face her while the cloth moved down across her abdomen, her muscles rippling with excitement and need beneath her touch.

"Your cat is wanting tonight," Win said before she knelt down between Alix's strong legs to pleasure her.

Alix's feral growls echoed in the shower when her orgasm tore through her body. When her body was sated, Alix lifted Win to her feet and crushed her mouth with a searing kiss.

"Enough for now, but there will be more once we finish," Alix said as Win looked at her with pleading eyes.

They finished showering and dressed for the evening, Alix in jeans and a black t-shirt while Win dressed in her leathers. "Don't forget the necklace tonight," Alix reminded her.

Win took the necklace from the box, wrapped it around her neck, and then turned to Alix to secure the straps.

Alix turned Win's body to face her and smiled.

"Makes you even sexier," she growled. She leaned in to kiss Win, but found she could not make contact with her lips. "Very effective too, I might add."

"Too effective," Win said with a pout.

"Not if it helps to keep you alive tonight."

Win finished lacing her boots and then retrieved her revolver from the case. She removed and inspected each of the bolts, then slid them back into the chambers. Alix picked up the sheath holding her sword, careful not to make contact with the silver blade or handle, and handed it to Win.

Win slid the sheathed blade securely into place behind her back and checked to ensure the hilt was in perfect position.

Alix pulled Win's hair back into a short ponytail and tied it with a strip of leather. "Damn you're sexy," she stated when she looked at her lover.

"Are we ready?"

Alix looked at the clock. "Almost," she answered and pulled Win in for a hungry kiss, defying the searing pain from the silver.

"Now I'm ready," she grinned. "Let's roll."

†

Lucia stopped by on her way to the club. "I just wanted to wish you good luck, and make sure you have me on speed dial if you need me."

"I hope to God we won't need your services tonight," Devin said, "but yes, we both have you programmed into our phones."

Lucia shuffled her feet, worried for her friends. "I

166

will gladly buy drinks of celebration tonight, if you'll stop in at the club."

"You can bet we'll be there," Devin promised. "Have plenty of JD ready and waiting."

Lucia felt tears forming in her eyes, so she hugged both her friends and left before they could begin to flow. "Hurry home safely," she said, and fled the house.

Devin's eyes followed her until she rode off the property, and then she turned to Tia. "One more dose of tea for good measure?" she asked.

"It certainly can't hurt," Tia answered and started the water.

†

When Devin heard the SUV approaching, she took Tia in her arms for a long kiss. "No matter what happens tonight, remember how much I love you, and that I am proud of the woman you have become."

"I love you too. Now let's go kick some ass."

Devin chuckled and followed her lover out the door. The wind had picked up considerably, causing the trees to sway briskly, and she hoped it would die down before Win had shooting to do.

As Devin climbed into the SUV behind Tia, Win turned to them. "It seems there are several storms brewing tonight. Are we ready?"

"Yes, let's do this," Tia stated, feeling confident. She entwined her fingers with Devin's and felt her heart pounding when Devin's wolf began to rise to ascension. "I love you," she whispered and kissed Devin's lips.

"I love you too," Devin answered.

"I don't believe we've seen another living soul in five minutes," Alix said. The streets were eerily empty.

"The temperature is dropping and the natives stay inside if it drops below sixty," Devin joked to ease some of the tension she felt building inside the vehicle. "It will be a great night for a run later my friend," she said to Alix.

"That it will," Alix agreed, and stared at the empty street ahead.

When they arrived at the small building at the end of Canal Street, they parked in a secluded spot. They had arrived earlier than planned, but it gave them an opportunity to find where Simon and his enforcers were located. It was easy for Alix and Devin to locate them and Devin hoped that Anthony's group would be overly confident of their powers and not concerned with the scent of the wolves.

The heat emitting from Devin and Alex had drastically increased while their bodies surged with adrenalin in anticipation of the fight, and they decided to go ahead and shift to be prepared for Anthony's arrival. They stepped out of the darkened vehicle to undress, and once they had shifted, Tia and Win joined them.

The wind had died down and the temperature continued to fall. Tia stood beside the wolf, her hand buried in the thick coat, and the cat sat patiently in front of Win, her eyes scanning the surrounding area. A ground fog began rolling in off the water, staying low and adding to the surreal quiet of the night.

Devin's wolf scented Marcus and Lord Jordan's presence, and she gazed off in their direction. All the observers were in place and ready, now they just needed their prey to arrive.

Tia felt a strange buzzing in her head followed by a familiar voice. "I am with you Tia, do not be afraid." Her

Grandmother spoke inside her head. "I will send you all the energy I can, and I will block Anthony when he tries to enter your mind. You can concentrate on sending all your power through the spell. We will do this together."

"Yes, Grandmother," Tia whispered.

The wolf's sharp hearing heard her soft whisper, and she turned her head to lick Tia's hand with her warm tongue. Tia stood straighter and she took a step forward.

"It is time."

Chapter Twelve

Time passed quickly while they waited for Anthony and his wolves. Their senses were on full alert, and Tia felt Devin's wolf tense and flex her muscles.

Win felt the low growl coming from the cat while Tia spoke. They stepped from the darkness into the open lot next to the building, and faced the north. Before their eyes saw them, they felt the tingle of the approaching enemy.

The hackles on Devin's wolf rose when she smelled the scent of the Weres that had dishonored her species and threatened her pack. Her low growl rumbled from deep inside her while she left Tia's side and stepped forward as, suddenly, forms appeared through the fog. Anthony was flanked by one wolf to his right and two on his left, the best alignment for their plan. Then the plan suddenly changed when a second vampire stepped out from behind Anthony, standing to his right, overloading Devin's side.

"What the fuck," Win cried. "Where did he come from?"

"Another vampire," Tia said. "This certainly changes

things a bit."

Lord Jordan turned to face Marcus who looked on in horror when one of their clan stepped from behind Anthony. "What is this?" he snarled.

"James," Marcus hissed. "That greedy bastard has taken up with Anthony."

"You will deal with this," Lord Jordan stated. "A traitor from our clan cannot be allowed."

Marcus nodded his head with understanding and stepped away from Lord Jordan. He blurred and disappeared.

The fog licked up to waist level, giving the enemy the appearance of floating toward Devin's group. The wolves were large as they had feared, and they approached with arrogance and self-confidence bolstered by Anthony's enchantment.

Win's heart beat loudly against her chest when she saw the glistening fangs of the second vampire. Her mind rapidly analyzed the situation and she looked at Tia. "I will do my best to take them both."

Tia simply nodded. "We can do this," she said to bolster the group's confidence.

Anthony's group had scented their presence and approached swiftly. When they were within thirty feet of Tia and her group, Anthony stopped. His human form was gorgeous, his skin and features looked like chiseled marble to Tia. His eyes glowed, flames of excitement dancing deep in their depth while he glared at them. Tia could easily see how his allure brought in many followers. She could feel the endorphins he emitted even from this distance, and his form appeared to grow before her eyes while he took in their presence.

Anthony chuckled, a chilling sound to their ears, and

lifted his arms out to his sides. "Is this the best the great and powerful Lord Jordan could come up with?" he asked, his cold voice chilling Tia to the bone. "Two Weres and two human women," he taunted.

He paused when he picked up Tia's scent. He cocked his head and lifted his face to a light breeze as he drew in a deep breath.

"Let me stand corrected, one woman and a witch," he snarled with obvious pleasure. He locked eyes with Tia. "We could do this the easy way, and you could join me and your pets could go free." His voice rang out with a deep, sensual tone. He gave Tia an alluring smile.

"You and I could do great things together."

"Ignore his taunts and begin weaving your spell, I have him blocked." Ella spoke from inside Tia's mind.

Tia glared, fury flashing in her eyes. "Not in a million years," she growled as she strode forward to meet Anthony. "This is my town." Her mind formed the spell and she locked eyes with the powerful vamp.

Devin saw a blur approach from her left and scented Marcus before he appeared next to her.

"I will deal with the vampire," he hissed to her. "He's one of our clan and he will receive my wrath."

Devin breathed a sigh of relief and she stepped wider to allow Marcus nearer to Tia.

"Ah, now this is more interesting," Anthony, replied when Marcus stepped beside Tia.

They had closed the distance between them considerably and when the male wolves began to spread out, Win drew her revolver and let fly her bolts. The battle had begun.

Anthony swatted the bolt aimed at him with the ease he would a fly, sending it safely away and his head tilted back with a roar of laughter. "Really? Is this all you have?" he sneered arrogantly and resumed his laughter.

His rogues weren't so fortunate. Win's aim held true and she hit all three, the first with a shot through his heart. He whimpered once before collapsing to the ground. That evened the odds just as they had hoped. Win was feeling better with each passing second at how perfectly their plan was working. She hit the second wolf on his front shoulder, causing considerable pain to run through his body from the poisonous silver. His jaws snapped the air wildly until he managed to locate and pull the bolt from his body. Alix moved in quickly to engage him in battle.

Win's final bolt landed squarely in the third wolf's belly and he struggled in agony to remove it before Devin could approach. Devin was too fast for him and she pounced before he could remove the bolt.

The wolf in front of Alix was the largest she had ever seen and the fury of his pain from the bolt made his eyes glow red when she advanced on him. They both reared on hind legs, locked together as teeth and claws flashed in the night. Alix realized a moment too late that her exposed flank was a prime target. The wolf stopped lunging for her throat and his teeth found purchase in her flank, ripping a large gash down her side. She bit back a cry of pain, fearful it would distract Win from her task, and dropped down on all fours while the smell of her blood filled the air. *I have failed you, Win,* her mind projected when she turned back to face the oncoming wolf.

Win dropped the revolver to the ground, the clanking of heavy metal ringing in her ears. Ferocious growls and cries of pain filled the air. She could not allow the sounds to distract her concentration while the battle raged around her and her hand instinctively reached for the hilt of her sword, pulling it in slow motion from its sheath. The flash of the silver blade in the moonlight was reflected in Anthony's eyes, and for a brief second, Win thought she saw a flash of fear in his fiery eyes as his laughter fell silent. The look quickly transformed into rage, and his face contorted into his true image, one that was as hideous as his human face was beautiful. Win had seen this before and it did not prevent her from moving forward while she lifted the glowing blade above her head.

Tia felt the power growing inside her more strongly than she had ever experienced before while the spell wove through her mind, and when she glimpsed Win drawing her sword, she heard her grandmother's voice again in her head.

"Now!" Ella cried out. "Send him to hell where he belongs."

Tia used all of her strength to cast the spell onto Anthony, continuing to chant the words in her mind while the spell began to bind him. He slowed and his eyes glittered with rage and fear when he realized he had underestimated her abilities. Tia sent the last bit of power she could muster, and Anthony froze in midstride. Tia watched while Anthony's eyes shifted to witness the oncoming blade in disbelief.

With a blood-curdling yell, Win used all of her force to separate Anthony's head from his body.

Marcus had rushed the younger vampire, driving him away from the swing of Win's blade. He easily overwhelmed the vamp and ripped his head from his body with a powerful twist.

"You will no longer disgrace our clan," Marcus growled, while the vampire started to smoke and then broke into flames.

The decapitation broke Anthony's enchantment on the wolves and the wolf Devin was fighting hesitated briefly when the spell was broken, allowing her to lunge at him and deliver a killing blow. Her razor sharp teeth ripped out his throat, blood spraying through the air until he crashed to the ground, blood pouring from his devastated throat to soak the pavement. She turned her head to the right just in time to see Tia falling to the ground.

Win had aimed such a strong blow against Anthony that his head sailed ten feet from his body, his eyes still wide open with a look of terror. When his corpse began to smoke, she pivoted to find Alix embroiled in battle with the much larger wolf. Blood, hair, and saliva flew through the air while the two combatants fought, neither gaining an advantage until the form of Devin's wolf flew through the air smashing into the wolf's side, driving him to the ground, and she stood straddling his body. The wolf knew immediately that he was defeated and rolled onto his back into a posture of submission, his eyes begging Devin's wolf for mercy. Tonight she had none. Her battle frenzy rushed through her wolf as her teeth closed on his neck and ripped out his throat with fury. Then she lifted her muzzle to the air in a howl of rage and victory, the blood of the defeated running down her neck.

Win's eyes watched in horror when Alix's big cat stumbled and fell to the ground. She desperately tried to crawl a few steps closer to her lover, but the cat's energy was rapidly fading. Alix had taken a serious bite to her flank and was losing blood rapidly. The cat's coat did not provide the protection from teeth and claws that a wolf's thick fur did. Win's heart sank when she saw how badly Alix's flank had been ripped open. Win knew she would not have the ability to change back to human form and that only immediate medical attention could save her lover. She rushed to Alix's side, the silver sword clanging to the ground when it slipped from her hand, and she collapsed to her knees.

Tia was exhausted but managed to stand and pull her phone from her pocket to dial Lucia. "We need you to meet us at our place now, with your medical kit." It was all she could say when Lucia answered, before she stumbled and fell.

Simon and Lord Jordan appeared in the darkness from where they had observed the battle. Devin spun around when she scented their approach, the battle rage still overwhelming her, but Simon reached her mind. "It's over, little sister. You won, but your friend is badly injured."

The wolf's head snapped around to see Tia falling and she rushed to her aid. Devin transformed while she sped to Tia's side.

"Help Alix," Tia murmured, lifting an exhausted arm to point to their fallen friend. "Lucia will be waiting for us at home."

The big cat was panting rapidly when Devin approached and she could feel her adopted sister's pain. "We have to get her to our place so Lucia can stop this bleeding. Now, Win," she shouted to snap a stunned Win out of her shock.

"Simon, help me get her into the back of the SUV," Devin called.

When Simon reached to pick her up, the cat hissed at him. Devin looked at Win. "You have to tell her it's all right for us to move her. She will only respond to you."

"Relax, baby. Devin and Simon are going to take care of us now, so let them carry you." Win spoke softly to Alix.

They carefully lifted the cat from the ground and

carried her to the vehicle.

Marcus raced ahead of them and lifted the gate to make room for the cat. Simon and Devin laid her gently on the carpet and Win jumped in beside her. Devin handed her the t-shirt she had worn. "Keep pressure on the wound with this and I'll get us there as fast as I can."

Devin closed the gate and looked at Simon. "Will you care for Tia and bring her home?"

"Yes, I'd be honored. I'll have my men perform the cleanup, and I will bring her home."

"Thanks," she answered, and ran to the driver's side. She raced out of the parking lot.

"Please God let us be in time," Devin prayed aloud while the large SUV barreled through the empty streets.

†

Another SUV raced to the lot driven by one of Simon's pack. Simon lifted Tia into his strong arms and placed her inside the vehicle, carefully buckling her into her seat. "Hang on for a minute and let me give my men instructions. Then I will take you home."

Tia nodded, too numb and exhausted to form any words.

Simon quickly instructed his men to assist with the cleanup and then head for home. He spoke quickly to Marcus and Lord Jordan, agreeing to keep them updated on Alix, and then ran back to the vehicle. Tia was unconscious, scaring him briefly, until he placed his fingers on her neck and found a strong, steady pulse. He realized she had passed out from exhaustion. He put the SUV in gear and drove away as quickly as he could. He smiled when his saw Tia's hands

177

locked onto the hilt of Win's sword.

†

"I have to go," Lucia said to a panicked Kaitlin when she got Tia's call.

"What's wrong? Who's hurt?" Kaitlin asked.

Lucia shook her head. "I don't know. Tia just told me to meet them at home."

"Go, and I will see you soon."

Kaitlin called George over to the bar while Lucia raced to her bike. The weather had kept the crowd to a minimum, so she and George would let the crowd know that there was an emergency and they needed to close the bar. George would help close the bar down and drive Kaitlin home.

†

Lucia arrived home but there was no sign of her friends, so she raced up to her apartment to get all the medical equipment she could carry and then ran to Devin and Tia's house. She was surprised when she flew through the door to find Marie sitting at the kitchen table.

When Marie saw the terrified look on Lucia's face, she knew something had gone wrong. "What happened?"

"I don't know. Someone has been injured, but I don't know who or how bad." Lucia was on the verge of tears.

"Lucia," Marie called her name loudly. "You need to be calm and keep your head and wits about you. Concentrate on your medical training."

"You're right, Marie, thanks. Will you help me clear

178

this table and get these supplies set up?"

"I've got the table, you handle your equipment."

Lucia was certain that there would probably be gashes from teeth and claws so she pulled out thick pads of sterile gauze and suturing equipment. She rummaged through her bag to determine if she had anything for pain if needed.

"I'm going to put on some boiling water for tea. Tia will be exhausted when she arrives." Marie hoped that her young student wasn't the one injured.

Headlights flashed through the window when the SUV slid to a stop only a few feet from the front door. Devin raced to the back of the vehicle.

"Hold the door," Lucia told Marie. She flew past her and ran to meet Devin.

Devin's eyes flashed with fear when Lucia arrived. "It's Alix. She has a serious wound and is losing a lot of blood."

Lucia's heart raced when she saw the amount of blood coating the carpet in the rear of the vehicle. "Let's get her inside now," she said to Devin.

"Let me carry her, it will be faster than two," Devin said.

Win jumped from the back of the vehicle and Devin reached inside to lift Alix as gently as she could. She could hear the erratic heartbeat when she lifted the cat in her arms and rushed inside. "Be strong, my friend," she whispered into the soft coat of the cat.

"Place her here on the table," Lucia instructed.

Devin gently eased the cat onto the table and Win gasped at the front of Devin's body. Alix's blood covered Devin's chest and arms. Devin did a double take when she saw Marie in the kitchen. "Marie, will you see to Win please?" she asked.

"Yes, but let me get you some clothes first," Marie said then disappeared into the bedroom, returning moments later with a pair of jeans and a t-shirt. She also carried a damp washcloth. "Let me get some of that blood off you." She quickly wiped Devin's chest and arms while Lucia examined the cat.

Devin dressed and rushed back to the kitchen table. She saw the concerned look on Lucia's face while she studied the cat's wounds.

Her injuries looked even worse under the bright kitchen lights and Devin feared for her friend's life. She watched while Lucia finished her examination of the wound and placed a thick mound of gauze over the cat's flank. "Come here, Devin, and keep pressure on this while I get my supplies to stitch her up. We have to stop the bleeding."

Devin put pressure on the gauze and watched while the blood began to seep through the sterile white cotton. "Was there an artery hit? Why is there so much blood?"

"Her artery was barely missed but she has too much adrenalin coursing through her and her heart is pumping too hard," Lucia explained. "We have to slow it down or she will bleed out before I can get a stitch into her."

Marie had poured a large glass of whiskey for Win and was coaxing her to drink it to calm her nerves.

"Win, I need you now," Devin growled and Win came running while Devin hooked a chair with her foot and dragged it into place next to the cat's head. "You need to calm Alix, and get her heart to slow down, or we are going to lose her. She has too much adrenalin flowing through her veins from the fight."

Win sat in the chair and placed her head next to the big cat while she stroked her neck and whispered soothing words to her lover.

Devin could hear the cat's heart rate begin to slow, and it brought hope back to her. With her head bent over the cat, she felt something trickle into her eyes. She wiped her face on her shoulder and she found it was her own blood. She'd been too busy with all the commotion, to realize she was injured.

Lucia looked up at her to find she had a gash just to the right of her left eye, a wound that might also need stitches, but right now Lucia had more than she could handle with Alix.

"Marie, I need you to bring a stack of the sterile pads and a roll of the Kerlex, the sticky looking gauze."

Marie quickly found what Lucia had requested. Lucia handed her a bottle of Betadine. "Soak one of those pads and clean Devin's wound and then make a pressure bandage with the remainder and wrap it tightly around her head to stop her bleeding. We have way too much blood flowing in here and it's unnerving my wolf."

Lucia lifted the bandage Devin was holding against the cat's flank to find the blood flow had reduced significantly. "That's working, Win, keep soothing her cat." She saw the gleam of silver around Win's neck and growled. "Lose that silver around your neck, you are safe here." She watched while Win took off the necklace and placed it in her lap. Then she looked up at Devin. "Let Marie tend to you while I start suturing."

Lucia's brows knit together with concern as she examined the wound. Alix had lost a large amount of blood and her cat was too weak to heal herself. She had to seal the wound and then come up with a plan to get fresh blood into her system. Lucia knew Win's blood was not an option, because Alix's Were metabolism would reject the human blood. She grimaced when she looked at Devin. Lucia wasn't certain if Were blood from a different species would be healthy or harmful, but the options were slim. If she didn't act soon, Alix would die.

The door crashed open when Simon carried Tia into the house. Devin's wolf snarled when she found her lover in another Were's arms.

"Mine," she growled. Her protective instincts caused her wolf to fight for dominance and it took all of her focus to hold her wolf at bay.

"Relax, Devin, she's just exhausted," Simon told her.

"Put her on the bed," Marie instructed and she pointed him in the direction of the bedroom. Then she ripped the Kerlex from the roll to finish Devin's bandage.

Marie left her at the table and she moved back to the kitchen and made the tea Tia desperately needed. She also handed a mug to Devin. "I'll be right back."

Devin watched while she disappeared into the bedroom and Simon re-entered the room. She downed the bitter tea.

"Is there anything I can do?" he asked.

"Find someplace open with food and bring lots of it," Lucia replied. "It's going to be a long night."

Simon nodded and left the house.

Lucia looked at Devin and then at Win. "We have some decisions to make. Alix needs blood, and she needs it soon."

"No problem," Win stated, and placed her arm on the table.

"That won't work," Lucia replied. "Her body will reject human blood."

"What then?" Win asked.

Lucia turned her attention to Devin. "Alix needs Were blood. I'm not sure if yours will be accepted either, but we have to try or she will die. Her cat is not strong enough to heal her wounds."

"Let's do it," Devin answered, holding out her arm.

"We have to move her first. Alix needs to be at a lower level from you so gravity will help with the transfusion. "I'm only a medical student, so I don't have all the supplies I need to do this the right way." There was a note of nervousness in her voice while she surveyed the room. "The couch, we need to get her to the couch."

Devin carefully lifted the cat and carried her to the couch, followed closely by Win who resumed stroking the cat's head and talking to her in soft whispers.

"Grab one of the barstools," Lucia requested while she pieced together large IV tubing that she prayed would suffice for a transfusion line.

Devin retrieved the stool and sat on it, waiting while Lucia was deep in thought as she planned the process. Devin looked down to see the cat's tongue licking Win's hand, and an idea struck her like a lightning bolt. "Marie, come quick," she called out.

Marie who was watching over Tia rushed from the bedroom. "What?" she cried looking around the room.

"Tea, we need more of your tea," she said. "Warm but not hot, so Alix can lap it from Win's hand."

"Got it," Marie replied and rushed into the kitchen.

The door opened again and Kaitlin rushed through, followed closely by George. She looked at Devin and shrugged. "I'm sorry, I couldn't keep him from coming in to see what was going on."

George stood in shock, the color draining from his

face, looking from Devin to the black panther lying on her couch and back to Devin.

"What the hell?" he cried and stumbled backwards.

Devin looked at Kaitlin. "We're a little tied up here. Will you take George to your place, pour him a tall glass of Jack, and tell him what is going on?"

"Yeah," Kaitlin answered, letting out her breath. "Is everyone going to be okay here?"

"I hope so," Devin replied.

"I'll check back in later, but holler if you need anything." Kaitlin pushed a staring George back out the door.

Lucia went to work, inserting one end of the IV line into Devin's left arm and clamping it off once she had positive blood flow. Then she knelt beside Win and began to palpate one of the cat's front legs trying to find a suitable vein. "I know you can hear me and understand what I'm saying, Alix," she said. "I will be inserting a needle into your leg and it will be uncomfortable for a short time."

The big cat tried to lift her head and fixed her eyes on Lucia. Glazed with pain, it was apparent she was communicating with Lucia.

"Hold her leg still for me, Win," she requested. "She is horribly dehydrated, but I think I found a usable vein."

Lucia took a breath and slowly inserted the needle into what she hoped was a viable vein. When the backflow of blood slowly crept into the IV line, she released the breath she was holding. "Cross your fingers this works." She released the clamp on the line.

They watched while Devin's rich, dark blood filled the tube and entered the cat's leg. The cat trembled when Devin's heated blood reached her veins. Marie approached carrying the tea, handing it to Win while Lucia gently held the cat's leg in place.

Win poured a small amount of the tea into her palm and held it to the big cat's muzzle. Her tongue snaked out to lick the warm fluid from her hand and she promptly sneezed. Win chuckled. "I know it smells and probably tastes foul, but it will help, so drink."

Devin felt Tia stirring in the bedroom. "Marie, will you check Tia?"

Marie nodded and walked into the bedroom. Tia was sitting up on the edge of the bed. "You need more rest," Marie said, urging her to lie back on the bed.

"No, Marie, Devin needs me." Tia stood. Her head swam when the exhaustion threatened to overwhelm her, but she reached for Marie's hand. "Please take me to her."

Marie nodded and helped her into the living room. Tia sat on the loveseat and looked around the room. "How is she doing?"

Lucia looked up at her. "She's holding her own for now. Her cat is too weak from blood loss to heal her wound so we hope a dose of Devin's blood will give her a jump start."

Tia's eyes rested on Devin. "How does your head feel?"

"I'm fine," Devin said. "It will be healed before Lucia can poke me with her needle."

Lucia grinned at her friend, happy she was safe. "What happened tonight?"

"Anthony is a threat to us no more," Devin replied. "Our plan worked almost perfectly, except for Alix being injured."

Lucia nodded and understood no more questions were welcome.

Devin's eyes took in Tia and then landed on Marie. "I

think we could use more tea," she said.

Even Tia failed to complain when Marie delivered steaming mugs of the green tea. She lifted her mug to her lips and drank it down without argument.

Simon returned carrying bags of Chinese food and placed them on the kitchen counter. He looked into the living room to see the transfusion taking place and cocked his head at Devin. "Do you think that's wise?"

"We had no other choice," she replied.

"That's all we can do." Lucia removed the needle from the cat's leg after clamping the line, and then removed the needle from Devin's arm. The needle mark on Devin's arm closed and only a tiny purple bruise remained. Even that would fade in minutes. She lifted the sterile gauze from the wound. The bleeding had subsided, but there was no sign of the wound healing. She had hoped to see some sign that the skin was regenerating.

Lucia looked at Marie. "Get some food into them please."

Devin stepped down from the barstool and joined Tia on the loveseat, wrapping an arm around her shoulders.

"What now?" Tia asked.

Lucia looked up at them. "Now we wait."

Simon assisted Marie with preparing plates and carried them in to Devin, Tia, and Win. Win shook her head, refusing the food until Simon's deep voice commanded her. "You will be no good to her if you do not keep your strength."

"I just can't eat," she cried.

"You can try," Devin stated. "Simon is right and he is the ruling Alpha, so eat."

Win sat on the floor next to Alix on the couch and placed her food on the coffee table. She picked through the food until she found a tempura prawn and took a bite. They were Alix's favorite, so she turned and offered her lover a bite. She held the tasty treat in front of the cat's muzzle with great hope.

Devin's heart ached when a single tear fell from the cat's eye and she turned away from the food. "It's too early yet." Devin's words sounded empty.

"Would you mind if I called our healer in?" Simon asked.

Lucia looked at him. "I would appreciate his professional opinion."

Simon stepped from the room to make the call. He was gone for several minutes and then returned to sit with them. "Ramon will be here in twenty minutes."

"Thank you," Devin replied. Even her normally ravenous appetite was absent while she worried about her friend. Finally, she pushed her plate away, picked up a bottle of water, and drained it.

Tia had barely eaten as well and looked like she would fall asleep in her plate at any moment. "You need sleep, my love," Devin told her.

"I want to stay with you."

"I promise to wake you in a few hours," Devin said as she stood to help Tia to her feet. "I'll be right back," she told Win and carried Tia to the bedroom. She tucked the covers around Tia. "I need you rested my love. Tomorrow is going to be a very long day if things don't go well tonight."

"I understand, Devin. Win will need me."

"Yes she will. We must give her hope. If I can, I'm going to try to get her to rest while Lucia and I keep vigil over Alix."

Devin sat on the edge of the bed and watched until

Tia slipped off to sleep. She knew how exhausted her lover was and feared it could take days before her strength would return to normal. She reached down to brush a strand of hair from Tia's face and whispered, "I love you."

When she returned to the living room, Ramon, Simon's healer, had arrived and was examining the cat with a grave look on his face. When he finished, he turned to Lucia. "You've done well and all you can for her right now. I wouldn't have done anything differently, but now it's up to her will to live and the strength of her heart."

Win broke down at his words and Devin took her in her arms. "Alix is strong and her cat will bring her through. You have to believe in her love for you." She brushed away Win's tears. "Will you lie down and rest for a while?" Devin was prepared for an argument from Win, but she surprised everyone by nodding her agreement. The emotional turmoil had taken a toll on Win.

"I promise I will wake you if anything changes."

"I trust you, Devin, but I will not leave her side," Win replied. "Let me sleep here for just a little while, then wake me please."

"Marie, will you please get some bedding from the guest room?" Devin asked.

"Yes, I will," Marie, answered.

Devin and Marie made a pallet for Win on the floor beside Alix. When Win stretched out, Devin followed Ramon and Simon from the room.

Once outside, Devin turned to Ramon. "Will she survive?"

Ramon shrugged his shoulders. "I really can't say. It all depends on her will to live."

Devin's frustration was obvious. "Is there nothing else we can do?"

Ramon shook his head. "Pray if you believe."

Devin walked them to the door. "Thank you for all your help."

"You're most welcome. After all that you ladies have done tonight, it is to you we owe thanks. You have my number if you need anything." Simon followed Ramon into the darkness.

Devin watched them drive away and then saw Kaitlin approaching from across the yard. "How is George?"

Kaitlin grinned. "He's passed out on my couch, but he'll be fine."

"There's food on the counter if you're hungry," Devin said as Kaitlin stepped inside.

"I couldn't eat right now, but thank you," Kaitlin replied. She smelled the coppery scent of blood and turned to see the blood on the kitchen table. "I can clean this up if you don't mind."

"I'll help you," Devin stated.

"No you won't. Go sit and rest," Marie instructed. "We will take care of this."

Devin nodded and walked over to the couch to sit with Alix, placing the cat's large head in her lap, gently stroking the soft coat. "Fight hard my friend," she whispered.

"Can I get you anything?" Lucia asked. "You need to drink to build your blood back up in case we need more."

"Water then, please," she answered.

Lucia walked to the refrigerator for two bottles of water and returned to sit on the stool next to Devin. She handed her a bottle and opened one for herself.

"You did great tonight, my friend," Devin told her when she took the water. "Your father would be proud."

"I hope it's enough," Lucia replied and took a long

drink.

Devin smiled. "It will be."

Kaitlin and Marie cleaned the kitchen first, and then the dining room table that was covered with congealed blood. Kaitlin opened a window to rid the room filled of the coppery smell of blood.

Devin stroked down Alix's back, feeling the strong muscles twitching under her touch while her heartbeat remained slow and strong. She watched the slow rise and fall of her side as she breathed slowly.

Chapter Thirteen

Kaitlin refused to go home. She did leave long enough to check on George who was snoring soundly while he stretched out on her couch. When she returned, Devin was trying to convince Marie to lie down with Tia for a bit of rest.

"I promise to wake you in two hours," she pleaded with the elder.

Marie shook her head. "I'm in no need of sleep. You should go snuggle your lover and keep her warm."

"I'm too restless to sleep and Tia needs her rest. The spell took all her energy and even your tea won't be enough tonight."

Marie nodded and smiled at her. "She worked the spell perfectly, didn't she?"

"You would have been proud," Devin said while her hand softly stroked the cat's neck. "She nailed him perfectly and Win sent his head flying a good ten feet with her blow."

†

"She did what?" Damien roared into the phone, his grip on the cell so tight the plastic case threatened to explode. Enraged by the news he was receiving, Damien, the Alpha of the Baton Rouge pack and Devin's older brother, released a growl from deep in his body as his wolf leapt to the surface.

"She honored your pack well," Marcus repeated. "Anthony and his rogues were defeated tonight, by our hunters, Devin and Tia." It suddenly occurred to Marcus that Damien was not aware of his sister's involvement.

"Back up and start this conversation over, Marcus," Damien growled.

Marcus remained silent for a few awkward seconds. "You did not know Devin was involved, did you?" he asked sheepishly.

"I had no fucking clue, and none of you bothered to inform me," Damien raged. "Tell me everything that happened."

Ten minutes later Marcus finished telling Damien about the events leading up to tonight's victory and Damien's rage flared into an inferno.

"None of you thought to give me a call?" he growled.

"I'm sorry, we assumed you would know or that Simon would have told you." Marcus was obviously flustered.

"Simon was in on this too?" he growled in disbelief. "I will fucking deal with him later. If you or Lord Jordan ever involves Devin or Tia in anything like this again, you damned well better notify me."

"You have our sincerest apology," Marcus said. "I promise they entered into this voluntarily."

"Wait, you said someone was hurt." Damien's fury

was beginning to calm.

"Alix Augustus, a werecat adopted by Harley. She and her partner, Win Weston, were the bounty hunters. Alix took a serious bite to her flank during the battle," Marcus explained.

"Will she survive?"

"I cannot answer that," Marcus replied.

"I will find out for myself," Damien said.

Tara, his mate, had sensed his distress and rushed to his side. "What's going on?"

"Lord Jordan sent Devin and Tia into battle against one of the most powerful vampires in the States with a pair of bounty hunters," he said through gritted teeth. His rage threatened to reach the boiling point again. "And no one, not Lord Jordan, Simon, or Devin, thought it necessary to contact me."

"Is she okay?"

"She's fine, but one of the hunters, a werecat, was seriously injured." Damien looked at his phone and punched the speed dial button for Devin.

Damien growled when he got her voicemail. "I'm going to New Orleans," he snarled and walked to his truck.

"Be safe, and go easy on them," she pleaded.

He wheeled and gave her a crushing kiss. "I can't promise you that, but maybe the drive will give me enough time to calm down. I will call you later."

†

Lucia slipped away long enough to return to her apartment, shower, and change clothes. When she returned to find Devin, Kaitlin, and Marie asleep in the living room, she crept closer to check on the cat's wound. She was surprised and delighted to find that the skin around the wound was trying to mend. She took a seat in a comfortable chair, and she too drifted off to sleep.

✝

Tia awoke from a dream with a start and tried to shake the cobwebs from her head. She could feel Devin calling to her from her dream, and she painfully climbed from the bed in search of her lover. She walked into the room to find everyone asleep and decided to remove the cushions from the back of the couch to slide in behind the cat to be close to Devin. She gently lay down next to the cat, and heard a soft purring when her hand stroked the cat's coat.

"We're all right here for you," Tia whispered, and placed her head next to the cat's on Devin's lap and fell promptly back to sleep.

Devin felt Tia's body next to her while she slept, and instinctively placed her arm on Tia's hip.

Another hour passed and Win woke and wiped the sleep from her eyes. Marie was the only one awake and she was watching Tia intently.

When Marie looked up to find Win awake, she placed a finger to her lips to silence her and then pointed to the couch where Tia and the cat lay sleeping, their heads in Devin's lap.

Win wiped an exhausted hand over her eyes to make sure what she was seeing was not part of her dream. Tia had her hand placed on the cat's back and it was glowing with energy. Somehow, Tia's magic was sending energy to Alix.

She looked back at Marie who was smiling. She

nodded her head and motioned for Win to come sit beside her to watch the miracle happening before their eyes.

"How long has this been going on?" she whispered quietly.

"About twenty minutes," Marie replied. "She's healing her somehow."

Tears flowed down Win's cheeks while she watched Tia smiling in her sleep as she softly ran her fingers through the cat's coat.

Lucia stirred and her eyes grew wide when she, too, saw what was happening. She looked at Marie who just shrugged.

Kaitlin's eyes flew open when she heard the crunching of tires in her driveway. Marie looked out the window to see Damien's truck pull into the drive.

"Uh oh." Marie stood and rushed out the door before Damien could come storming in. She met him halfway across the yard and stopped him in his tracks.

"My God, you're involved in this too?" he cried.

"Shush, now is not the time, my Alpha," she told him. "There is a miracle going on inside, but you cannot interrupt it by storming in there."

"What's going on?" he asked.

"Tia doesn't realize it, but she's healing Alix."

"What?"

"Come see for yourself, but don't wake them."

"Okay, I promise to be quiet." Damien followed her inside just as the first rays of sun were peeking across the horizon.

†

From the front stairwell leading up to Lucia's apartment, Elana, the beautiful vampire who had been sent to guard them, heard the news she had been waiting for and quickly left the premises to report in to Lord Jordan.

†

Devin stirred when her brother's scent reached her nose and she opened her eyes to find him staring at the couch. Everyone else in the room was looking at the couch, so she turned her head to see what was drawing their interest. When she saw the glow beneath Tia's hand, she smiled and knew her lover had found her healing powers.

They were all watching when the cat's form began to shimmer while she tried to shift.

"I better get a blanket," Marie muttered and left the room.

Damien sank into a seat beside Kaitlin while they maintained the vigil. Marie returned with a light blanket and placed it on the end of the couch.

Tia felt movement under her hand when the cat's muscles rippled and opened her eyes to find everyone watching her. "What?" she asked.

"Look at your hand, my love," Devin said.

Tia's eyes turned to see the glow and instinctively she jerked her hand away and the glow faded. She looked at her palm and then placed it back on the cat's side and the glow resumed. She looked up at Devin and asked, "How?"

Devin shook her head. "I have no clue, but it appears to be working."

It took several attempts but the cat finally transformed into human form. Tia placed the blanket over the

196

naked woman and then looked around the room.

Alix pulled the blanket around her body and painfully rose to a sitting position without uttering a word.

Win rushed to her and pulled her into an embrace. "You had us terrified," she said while she covered Alix's face with kisses.

"I'm starving," Alix croaked.

Marie walked to the kitchen followed by Lucia, who grabbed a bottle of water for Alix, while Marie heated Chinese leftovers.

Tia looked around the room to find several pairs of eyes still on her. "Oh hey, Damien."

Devin's head whipped around to face her brother. She had seen him enter, but his presence had not registered until Tia called his name.

"When did you get here?" she asked.

"Just a few minutes ago. Just in time to witness a miracle."

Tia was staring at her hand. "How did I do that?" she asked Devin.

Devin shook her head. "I don't know. I didn't realize you had healing powers."

"That makes two of us," Tia replied.

Alix drank the whole bottle of water and then turned to Tia. "I think I can help you out there," she replied to everyone's surprise. "I was dreaming when you curled up behind me, and when your hand touched my cat, I could feel energy flowing into my body. There was a woman, Ella was her name, and she told me she would help you heal me."

"Grandma," Tia replied. "She was with me last night too when we met Anthony, and she blocked him while I wove the spell."

"About that," Damien said with a frown.

"Now is not the time, Damien," Marie reminded him from the kitchen. "You can beat us all into submission later. For now, we will celebrate Alix's return to us and be happy."

Devin felt her brother's angry gaze when she looked at him, but he honored Marie's wishes.

Alix looked at Win. "Could you get my clothes from the SUV? I'm the only naked one here."

"Sit tight and I'll get them," Lucia replied while Kaitlin moved to the kitchen to help Marie dish up plates of food.

Win helped Alix to stand and walk to the bathroom. She took the clothes from Lucia to help Alix dress.

"Before you dress, can I take the stitches out?" Lucia asked. "I don't think you need them anymore and it won't take but a minute."

"Sure," Alix replied. "Thank you for tending to me. Thank you all." She had tears in her eyes.

†

"We're going to need more food," Devin said. "Would you drive me?" she asked Damien.

Damien nodded, understanding that this was Devin's way of taking his full wrath, saving her friends from the anger that was boiling inside him.

"We'll be back with beignets," Devin promised as she followed Damien out to his truck.

Tia looked at Marie. "How much trouble is she in?"

"Plenty, but if anyone can smooth things over with Damien, it's his baby sister."

†

Devin climbed into Damien's truck and, before he could start in on her, she explained. "I asked everyone not to call you, so I take full blame."

"That wasn't your call to make," he said with a growl. "Simon and Lord Jordan knew better."

"I made them promise as part of the deal," she answered. "You couldn't get involved without breaking Council Law."

"And you had to get involved why?" he asked.

"For several reasons. First, because my skills were needed. Anthony had promised his rogues control of our pack once he ruled New Orleans. You couldn't get involved since it was not a conflict directly related to our pack. Second, because Tia was needed, and I would never let her go alone into something so difficult."

"And so dangerous," Damien reminded her.

"There was no other choice, and if Alix and Win would have attempted the confrontation without us, it would have been suicide and a great loss to all our communities."

Damien backed the truck out of the drive while he considered Devin's responses. Devin could feel his anger and saw his white-knuckled grip on the steering wheel.

"I know it was wrong to not tell you, but I had to do this for the pack." She let out a deep sigh. "Not only because you are my Alpha and my brother, but if Anthony was successful, there would have been financial implications for the pack's business ventures as well."

Damien was slowly beginning to understand her reasoning, but he was still very angry with her and the others who had kept her activities secret from him.

"You brought great honor to the pack with your victory, but you risked too much," he said, his voice cracking with emotion.

"I risked what my heart told me was necessary," Devin pleaded.

"You have to promise me there won't be any secrets between us in the future," he told her. "I may not agree with you, but you are still bound to me by blood, and I am also your Alpha. I demand that respect from you."

"I am sorry," Devin said again when they reached the square and found a parking spot.

Damien met his sister at the front of the truck and hugged her tightly. "Please don't make me worry about losing you again."

Still wrapped in his strong arms, Devin looked up at her brother. "I won't, I promise."

"Don't make me send Lizard down to keep you two out of trouble," he teased.

Devin adored her young niece Elizabeth, whom she had nicknamed Lizard when she was a small child. She chuckled. "Lizard would be welcome at any time."

"She's going to be mad with me when she finds out I've come to see you this morning without her, but this was no situation for her to be in."

"How did you find out, anyhow?" Devin asked when he released her.

"Marcus called me to let me know the mission was successful."

"Damned vamp traitor." Devin smirked.

"He assumed, incorrectly, that I knew you were involved and called to praise your efforts."

"I am proud that you taught me to fight like you did," Devin said, and Damien smiled.

"Go ahead and place our order and let me call Tara to let her know everyone is safe, and I will join you in a few minutes. Oh, and Devin," he called, "place a big order, I'm hungry."

"Got it." Devin walked into the restaurant.

✝

The Chinese food disappeared and Marie made mugs of green tea for both Tia and Alix.

"Don't complain, just drink it," she instructed them. "I know you both think you are feeling fine, but you've released vast amounts of energy that must be replaced."

Alix picked up her mug and made a face at Tia. "C'mon put your big girl panties on," she teased and downed the tea.

Tia downed the contents and placed the mug on the table. "I must be hallucinating, that stuff is beginning to taste better."

"There's more if you want another cup," Marie replied.

"No, I believe I'll switch to coffee and wait on beignets," Tia answered.

The door opened and George came stumbling in rubbing his aching head. "I knew I smelled coffee. May I have a cup? My head is pounding."

"Kaitlin, if you will pour him a cup, I'll get George some aspirin," Tia replied.

Tia went to the bathroom for the medicine. When she returned, she handed them to George. She ran her hand across his forehead to remove his pain and any memories of what he had seen last night.

"Thanks Tia. I had the weirdest dream that there was a huge black panther lying on your couch." He was still rubbing his head.

"Well, you can see there's no panther on the couch. It must have been all the whiskey you drank last night," Kaitlin teased. "You wiped out my supply."

"I'm sorry," George replied. "I think I'll go home and shower. I'll drop off your mug later," he told Tia and left the house.

They watched him walk to his truck and Kaitlin turned to Tia. "He won't remember anything, will he?" Kaitlin said to Tia with a knowing smile.

Tia grinned back at her. "When he wakes up from his nap today, he won't even remember the dream."

"I think I'm in the same boat with George," Alix said. "I don't remember much from last night either."

"Probably best you didn't." Win was stroking her lover's face. "You gave us all a scare."

"Was there really a second vampire?" Alix asked.

"Yes, apparently one of Lord Jordan's clan had defected to Anthony's control. Marcus joined us and destroyed him," Win explained.

"What will happen since he killed one of his own?" Alix asked.

"I'm sure there will be some repercussions from the Council, but his actions were justified, and I was never happier to see a vampire when Marcus showed up. I have no idea how we could have handled a second vampire."

†

Everyone was sitting around the table, drinking

202

coffee and staring out the window when Damien's truck returned. They watched him as he and Devin carried in large bags filled with beignets.

"She's smiling, so that's a good sign," Marie remarked. She rose to pour two more mugs of coffee.

"I think I'm going to grab a beignet and run so you can have your family time," Kaitlin decided. "I'll check on you later."

Devin and Damien entered and placed the bags on the table. "It's good to see you again, Damien, but I'm going to head home," Kaitlin said. "It's been a long night."

"Thank you for watching over these women. I hope to see you again soon."

"You too." Kaitlin took a beignet. "Thanks for breakfast."

"You're welcome," Damien replied and he opened the door for Kaitlin. When he turned back to the table, he looked at Devin. "Do you think she would close the club down on Sunday night?"

"I don't know? We could ask. Why?"

"Because it's time you and your friends came home for a celebration," he answered. "We will have a feast on Sunday and you can all stay at the compound Sunday night."

Devin looked at Win. "Can you stay until then?"

Win looked at Alix who smiled at her with anticipation. "I don't see why not, we need some time to rest before we return home."

"If you don't mind, I would like Doc to examine you," he told Alix. "I'm not judging the care you gave her, Lucia, but he's treated werecats before."

"I'm not offended in the least." Lucia looked at Alix. "I think it would be a good idea."

"I would be thankful then," Alix replied. "You can doctor me anytime though, Lucia."

A blush rose to Lucia's cheeks. "Thanks."

Devin rested a hand on Lucia's shoulder. "Your father would have been proud of everything you did last night."

"Just don't feel like you need to test me anytime soon, okay?" she said with a wink to Alix.

"No problem," Alix replied. "I think I'll take things easy for a while."

"Will you stay for dinner?" Devin asked her brother.

"I'd like too, but I have a celebration to plan," Damien smiled. "I have other pack business to attend to as well."

"Okay then. I think it's time for some red meat," Devin announced.

"Oh hell yeah," Alix agreed eagerly.

After they finished off the beignets and three pots of coffee, Alix stretched and Win could see the weariness in her lover's face.

"If you will excuse us, I think it's time for us to head back to the hotel for a nap," Win said.

"I think we could all use some rest," Marie said. "Damien, will you drop me off on your way out of town?"

"I'd be honored," he answered.

"Plan to be back here around four and we will have a great meal," Devin told the group. "I'll hit the grocery and come back for a nap."

"Let me take you to the grocery before I leave so you don't have to wait on a delivery," Damien suggested.

"You have a deal, my Alpha," Devin replied.

"We'll drop Marie then, so she can check on Rue Paul," Win offered.

Devin turned to Lucia. "Will you tell Kaitlin what we

have planned and let her know we will deliver plates for her and George to the club? Also, ask her about Sunday if you would please."

Lucia nodded and walked out of the house. Alix, Win, and Marie followed her out to the SUV. "Would you like to go to the store with us?" Devin asked Tia.

"No, if you don't mind. I will pick up around here and lie down for a while."

"Are you okay?" Devin asked when she embraced her.

"Just tired," Tia replied.

"Leave the kitchen and I'll straighten it up when I get back." Devin kissed her softly. "I will be back soon."

"It was good to see you and I'm very proud of what you did," Damien told her when he hugged Tia. "Get some rest and I will see you Sunday, unless you want to come earlier."

"Thank you, Damien," Tia replied.

†

Damien and Devin left for the grocery store while Tia straightened the house before taking a hot shower. She was weary to the bone but she had never felt more confident of her abilities.

"Thank you, Grandma," she said after she had slipped between the cool sheets.

When they returned from the grocery, Damien helped his sister carry the groceries into the house. "Remember, no more secrets," he said and held her close. "I love you, baby sister."

"I love you too. Hugs and kisses to Tara and the kids

for me please."

"Lizard will be so excited for you to come home," he replied with a grin. "Me too."

"I'll call you in a day or so to finalize the plans," she promised and then walked him out to the truck. "Drive safe." "Always," he promised and pulled away. Devin walked back inside to check on Tia before getting the steaks ready to cook later in the day. She stepped inside the door of their bedroom leaning against the doorframe and simply stood there for several minutes watching Tia sleep. With a deep sigh, she pushed away from the door and returned to the kitchen to finish her tasks.

Chapter Fourteen

When the alarm sounded for Devin to wake and begin preparing for dinner, Tia still slept soundly. Devin crept from the bed and made her way in to the kitchen to start baking the potatoes she had wrapped in foil. She tossed a salad and made a pot of tea to go with the meal. She pulled a cold Abita and popped the cap, taking a long drink of the icy beverage. Devin looked out the front window to see Lucia setting up the grill and placing lawn chairs in the shade. She took another Abita from the refrigerator and walked outside.

The afternoon sun was brilliant and the cold front that had descended on New Orleans the previous night had moved through, taking much of the normal humidity with it when it moved east. Lucia looked up to see her approaching.

"I thought I would get a head start for you," she said when she took the offered beer. "Thanks."

"Thank you, for everything you did last night and today."

"I was glad to be here," Lucia answered.

Devin sat in a chair beside Lucia. "I'm so glad last

night is over and maybe things will be back to normal soon."

Lucia chuckled. "Do you really think life will ever be like it was for you before you met Tia? Do I need to remind you that you are paired with a spell binder? I fear this will be your new normal, my friend."

Devin let her words sink in for several seconds, and then she lifted her head to see Tia approaching across the yard. She smiled. The sun shone down on Tia, ringing her head with a golden halo as she walked. "I'll take this kind of normal any day."

"Am I interrupting?" Tia asked.

"We were just talking about how beautiful the day has been," Lucia replied.

Tia sat in Devin's lap, her hand running through her lover's raven black hair. "What do I need to prepare inside?"

"The potatoes are in the oven, the salad is chilling, and the tea is steeping," Devin answered. "Other than boiling some corn, we should be ready. Do you want to eat outside?"

Tia looked over to Lucia. "I think that would be nice, don't you?"

Lucia nodded. "This weather is too nice to be inside."

"Do you want us to set up a table while you start the fire? The others will be here soon?" Tia asked.

They heard the approach of a vehicle and turned to see the SUV pulling into the drive. "You were saying?" Devin teased.

"Now that the others are here, I'll sit back and watch you and Lucia prepare the table."

Devin smiled at her lover. "I think that's the perfect plan."

Win parked and she, Alix, and Marie stepped from the vehicle. Alix looked amazingly healthy given the fact she had been at death's door only twelve hours earlier. Alix opened the back gate and pulled out a cooler that she easily picked up and carried to where the others were sitting. She placed the cooler on the ground and opened it up to take fresh beer from inside.

"We thought some icy cold beer would taste good," Alix said as she handed one to Win, Marie, and Tia. "Are you two ready for another round?" she asked, looking at Lucia and Devin.

Lucia held her bottle toward Devin who tapped the bottle's neck against Lucia's and they drained the contents. "We are now," Lucia replied.

Alix chuckled and then she removed two more beers from the cooler and carried them to her friends. She eased herself down into a chair next to Devin.

"How are you feeling?" Lucia asked.

"Still a bit stiff, but otherwise great," she answered. "Nothing a few days rest won't cure. When do you plan to go to Baton Rouge?"

"I thought we might go up Friday, if Lucia will cover me a couple more days," Devin replied.

"No problem," Lucia answered.

"Would you mind if we came along then and brought Marie with us? I'll be ready for a good run in two days."

"The more the merrier," Devin said. She turned to Lucia. "Can you bring Kaitlin up on your bike Sunday morning?"

Lucia smiled brightly. "I'd love to."

"All settled then. If you'll let me up, I'll start the fire and set up the table," Devin told Tia.

Devin, Lucia, and Alix went to work lighting the fire and setting up the table for an outdoor dinner while Tia and Win watched them with interest. "Is she doing as well as she looks?" Tia asked.

"Remarkably so," Win answered. "I will be forever in your debt for what you did for her. I would be devastated if I had lost Alix."

Tia held her hand out to Win. "I understand completely. I would feel the same if something happened to Devin." Her eyes followed the movement of her lover. "I hope you'll take a long vacation before jumping into the next project. You two deserve some time together."

Win had also been watching the three Weres while they worked together. "We have no need to work for quite some time, but I'm sure the longing to hunt and do what we were born to do will call us again in the future."

"That is good news to hear."

"Last night scared the hell out of me," Win admitted. "I hope we never have a challenge like that again."

"If you do, call us," Tia declared.

Win's head whipped around to look at her. "Are you serious?"

"If you need extra help and we have the powers to assist, yes," Tia answered.

"Does Devin know what you think about this?"

Tia chuckled while she tore her eyes away from her beautiful lover. "I don't really think I need to answer that. Devin's Were. Also born for the hunt."

"Good point," Win agreed.

Marie had remained so quiet that Tia and Win had forgotten she was sitting next to them. "You'll have many more battles ahead of you."

"I know you're right," Win replied. "There never seems to be an end to evil."

Marie nodded and took another sip of her beer.

Tia sighed at the darkness of their mood. "We should

go put the corn on to boil and bring out dishes and utensils. It won't take long once Devin puts the steaks on to cook."

Win, Marie, and Tia walked into the house while Devin, Alix, and Lucia settled into their chairs and sipped beer.

When the sun slipped below the horizon, the friends sat down to a feast and enjoyed the meal while the darkness grew around them. Lucia turned on the lanterns placed on the table while Marie and Tia made plates for Kaitlin and George. She would deliver them when she went to assist Kaitlin at the club.

"Are you sure you don't want me to drop you off?" Win asked.

Lucia smiled at her offer. "No, I want to enjoy a few more minutes of this beautiful night," she said while she picked up the plates.

"Have a great night," Devin said.

"Thanks, you too," Lucia answered, and she slipped into the darkness and disappeared.

Devin sat back in her chair and Tia slipped her hand inside Devin's, entwining their fingers. She enjoyed watching the night sky and was lost in tracking a jet while it headed to the New Orleans airport when she felt a buzzing in her head. The others had sensed it too and were leaning forward in their chairs to see who was approaching.

"Vampires," Alix snarled.

"Relax, it's Marcus, and Elana," Devin replied.

They watched the two figures silently approaching them in the darkness. "Welcome," Devin said when they stopped next to the table. "Would you care for a cold beer?"

"That would be lovely," Elana replied, and her eyes glowed when she smiled at Devin.

211

"To what do we owe the pleasure of your visit?" Devin asked when she had handed them each a beer. "Would you care to sit?"

"We won't interrupt your relaxing evening for long. Lord Jordan wanted to ensure you were compensated for your efforts as agreed upon," Marcus answered. He moved forward to hand envelopes to Tia and Win. "Inside you will find your payments and a small sum for Marie and the healer for their assistance. Lord Jordan will also have a vehicle delivered for you tomorrow," he said to Tia.

"I have transportation," she replied.

"And he is painfully aware," Marcus stated. "He does not wish to see you unprotected from the elements and has purchased a vehicle for your protection."

Tia was speechless. Devin nudged her. "I think 'thank you' is appropriate for this moment," Devin teased her.

"We also need to thank you for helping us last night," Devin added.

"It was my duty, being Lord Jordan's second, to rid the traitor from our clan," he said.

"You did a great service to all of us," Win added. "We could have just as easily been toast, without your help."

Marcus nodded his acceptance. "I will pass on your appreciation to Lord Jordan. I also owe you an apology, Devin, for raising the ire of your Alpha. For that I am truly sorry."

"I've already dealt with that, and came out relatively unscathed, so apology accepted."

"Our clan and this community are in your debt," Marcus said. With a slight bow, he turned and began walking away.

"Thanks for the beer, handsome," Elana purred with a beautiful smile before she turned to join Marcus.

Devin could feel the heat rising deep within Tia, and she feared her lover would send a fireball at the vamp's retreating form. "Relax, she's just flirting."

Tia looked at her with a flash of anger in her eyes. "Mine," she growled aloud.

Devin chuckled at her lover. "If I didn't know better, I'd say you had a touch of Were in you."

When Tia had finally relaxed, she opened the large manila envelope to find several smaller envelopes inside and handed one to Marie, one to Devin, and another with her name on it. As promised, there was also an envelope with Lucia's name.

"You will find Lord Jordan to be very generous and appreciative of your skills," Win said when she handed Alix their envelope.

"Oh my goodness," Marie cried and she clutched a check to her chest. She held out the check for Devin and Tia to see that an amount of ten thousand dollars was written on the paper.

"That will buy a lot of doggie treats for Rue Paul," Tia teased.

"I'd say," Marie agreed and she fanned herself.

Tia opened her envelope next and then handed it to Devin who had also opened hers. Both had checks written for fifty thousand. "Holy shit," Devin cried, when she showed Tia her check.

"I guess I no longer have to worry about the pack paying for nursing school," Tia said.

"What we were able to do for Lord Jordan saved him much more than this, I promise you," Win said. "We have all earned every penny of it, too," she added.

"Put it to good use," Alix said as she stood and

stretched. "I think it is time for us to go," she told Win.

Devin looked up at her, still in shock.

"Come on and we will help clean up before we go." Alix offered her a hand.

"We can get this," Tia said.

"I know you can, but with five of us working it will be done in no time," Win replied.

They cleaned up and Tia and Devin walked them out to the SUV. "Call us late tomorrow if you'd like to get together for dinner," Tia said.

"We will," Alix, answered.

Win drove away and Devin turned to Tia. "Would you like to go help Lucia and Kaitlin, or stay at home and relax?"

"I'd love to go curl up with you, but I feel like we should go to the club. I feel we've neglected Kaitlin for too long," she said with a grin. "Besides, we can sleep in late tomorrow."

"Go get Lucia's check and you can take her outside and give it to her while I help Kaitlin. Just be ready to steady her on her feet when she opens it," she added with a grin.

"I will." Tia smiled and walked back into the house.

When she returned, she took Devin's hand and they enjoyed the beautiful night while they walked to the club. "I feel like I should share something with you that I told Win," Tia said.

"What was it?"

"We were talking about last night, and I told her to give us a call if they ever needed our help. I'm sorry I spoke without talking to you first."

Devin stopped walking and turned toward Tia. "There's no need to apologize. I would have told her the same."

"Really?" Tia was relieved that Devin wasn't angry.

"Mind you, I don't want to do battle like that every week, but if they needed us once in a while, I wouldn't mind."

"I love you," Tia said and she wrapped an arm around Devin's waist.

Devin kissed the top of her head and draped an arm across her shoulders. "I love you too."

†

They reached the club and found the lot packed. Business had returned to normal and the music blared when Devin pulled open the door and they walked to the bar. Kaitlin and Lucia were busy filling orders, so Devin stepped in and went to work while Tia walked to her booth.

"Hey, Boss," she said to Kaitlin when she looked up at her approach.

"Hey, Devin," Kaitlin answered with a huge smile. She looked up and saw Tia walking toward her booth, then resumed filling orders.

When the rush ended, Devin looked to Lucia. "Tia has something for you if you want to go see her and get it."

"What is it?" Lucia asked.

"Go find out," Devin replied and gently pushed her down the bar.

Kaitlin looked at Tia in the booth and Devin behind the bar. "Just like old times," she said.

They watched while Lucia walked into the booth and Tia handed her an envelope. She opened it and Devin thought Lucia was going to fall down in shock.

"What's that all about?" Kaitlin asked.

"Payment from Lord Jordan for her services last

night," Devin replied with a smile.

"I'm sure that will be a welcome surprise."

"Are you okay with closing the club on Sunday?" Devin asked.

"Yes, I wouldn't miss a chance to see the compound and meet more of your family," Kaitlin replied. "I'm sure New Orleans won't dry out in one night."

"The rest of us are driving up on Friday if you don't mind riding up with Lucia Sunday morning."

Kaitlin grinned widely. "I'm looking forward to that ride."

Later, after the last customer was ushered out the door, they all pitched in to close up for the night and walked home together.

Lucia was still grinning from ear to ear. "May I take you all to a late breakfast in the morning?"

"I think that could be arranged. What time?" Tia asked.

"Ten, unless we all fail to sleep in late," she answered.

"That sounds good to me. See you then," Kaitlin replied, and walked inside her home.

"Have a great night you two," Lucia told them and she bounded up her stairway.

Devin draped her arm over Tia's shoulder. "I guess you're stuck with me tonight," she said.

"I am so ready to curl up in your arms and sleep," Tia replied.

Still not fully recovered, Tia looked tired. When they undressed and slipped between the cool sheets, Devin pulled Tia into her warm body and held her close.

Chapter Fifteen

A soft knocking on their door woke Tia and Devin at nine the next morning. Devin climbed from the bed, slipped a robe around her body, and went to answer the door. A large man in a dark suit was standing at the door when she opened it and he asked, "Are you Tia?"

"No, hang on one second," Devin replied and walked back to the bedroom. "It's for you. Looks like one of Lord Jordan's men."

Tia slipped a robe on and followed Devin back to the door. The man smiled brightly at her. "Lord Jordan asked me to deliver these to you," he reported and handed her keys. When he stepped from the doorway, they saw a sleek black Infinity parked in the drive.

"That's my new car?" she asked the man.

"Yes ma'am it is. Is it not to your liking?" he asked worriedly.

"Are you kidding? That's the most beautiful car I have ever seen."

The man chuckled softly. "You will find the

registration and insurance information in the glove box. Enjoy your new ride." He walked to the SUV parked behind the car and they drove away.

Kaitlin was sitting at her kitchen table when she saw the man appear briefly and then saw Tia and Devin dressed in robes walking across the yard to a beautiful black car. She watched the SUV pull away and then went out to join them. "What on earth?" she asked.

"A gift from Lord Jordan so Tia doesn't have to get wet riding her bike," Devin teased while Tia slid behind the wheel.

"Oh, wow, this is gorgeous," Tia cried. "Loaded with all the bells and whistles too." Excitement glowed in her eyes.

Lucia too had witnessed the exchange and stepped out of her apartment. "So you're driving this morning, right?"

"Yes," Tia squealed.

"Let's go get showered and dressed. Then we can go for breakfast. We'll meet you two shortly," Devin told Kaitlin and Lucia.

They shared a hearty breakfast at the diner and then Tia took them for a ride. "This is really smooth," Devin said as they drove down some of the older streets in town that would normally jar her teeth.

"It handles like a dream too." Tia had a smile plastered to her face.

They returned home and went their separate ways. Tia and Devin walked into their home to catch up on some laundry and wait for Win and Alix to call about dinner.

"I think I'll call Lord Jordan to thank him for the car."

"That would be a good idea."

Bound

Tia made the call and then joined Devin on the couch, snuggling in next to her. "This has been a crazy week."

"Yes it has," Devin agreed. "Since you still have your phone, please call Damien, and let him know we'll be there Friday," she requested.

"Okay, my love."

Devin's sensitive hearing could hear Lizard's squeal over the phone when she heard that Devin and Tia would be home Friday.

"I think she's a bit excited," Tia said when she ended the call.

"I heard," Devin replied with a grin. "So what would you like to do this afternoon?"

"Watch a movie and eat popcorn with my mate," Tia answered.

Devin grinned at her answer. "You pop the corn and I'll see what I can find on TV."

Neither of them made it through the movie and were snuggled up on the couch when Tia's phone began ringing and woke them,

"Hey, this is Win," she heard when she answered the phone.

Tia stifled a yawn and spoke. "Hey, Win."

"Did I wake you from a nap?"

"Yeah, but that's okay. Neither of us made it through the movie we were watching."

"Alix and I would like to take you two and Marie back to Acme tonight if that's good with y'all," Win said.

"We can always eat great seafood. Is Acme okay with you?" she asked Devin. A huge grin was her answer. "Yep, that would be perfect. What time?"

"Alix is starving. Could we meet at six?"

Tia looked at the clock. "Oh yeah that will be fine. See you there."

✝

After gorging themselves with seafood and Cajun delicacies, they relaxed back in their seats. "What time do you want to head up to Baton Rouge tomorrow?" Win asked.

"Let's plan to meet at Marie's at ten," Devin replied. "That will put us there in time for lunch."

Win chuckled when she paid the bill. "That sounds good."

They exited the restaurant together and walked to the lot. When Tia clicked the key fob to unlock the car, Alix whistled. "Is this yours?"

"Yes, a gift from Lord Jordan," she answered.

"Sweet ride," Alix stated when she looked inside. "Well deserved," she added.

"Thanks," Tia replied as she slipped in behind the wheel. "See you tomorrow."

"Goodnight," Alix told her and closed the door.

Marie chuckled when they drove off. "I think Tia could get used to bounty hunting," she told them with a grin.

"She would be unstoppable," Win agreed. She took Alix's arm and they walked to the SUV.

✝

Tia made love to Devin with renewed energy when they returned home and then fell exhausted into Devin's arms after a final simultaneous release. She turned to find Devin watching her.

"Will our lovemaking always feel this intense?" she asked, nearly breathless.

"Always," Devin smiled. "It will be even more intense when we return to the compound."

"Why is that?"

"Because as a group, the females all respond to the surge of hormones that triggers us to go into heat, the signal of our mating season," she answered calmly.

"Will I be affected?" Tia asked.

"Not by the heat itself, but I will be ravenous for nearly a week, so I would recommend keeping lots of the green tea close by when it happens."

"I know we cannot procreate," Tia replied. "Will you be disappointed by not being a parent?"

Devin had often wondered about having a child and she had realized the sacrifice of mating with Tia and had gladly made her choice. "I don't think so. Besides, there are always little ones running around the compound. There will be plenty of opportunities to interact with them."

Tia looked up into Devin's eyes and asked, "Is there a chance I could get pregnant?"

Devin leaned back and looked at her in disbelief. "I honestly don't know. It is rare that two female Were can reproduce, but I'm not at all sure. There are always other means," she offered.

"Artificial, you mean?"

Devin chuckled. "Yes, I don't think Tara would appreciate you sleeping with her husband."

"Would Damien be a donor for us?"

"I would accept no other," Devin stated. "Our child would have to be of my blood."

"We have plenty of time to consider that later," Tia

replied. "I just needed to know if it was possible."

"Only time will tell," Devin answered, and kissed her lover.

✝

Devin's excitement grew when they were finally on their way to Baton Rouge. Until they were on the road, she hadn't realized how excited she was to return home. Her pulse soared when they made the turn into the compound and she saw Lizard come flying out of the house. Tia pulled into the drive and parked while Win pulled up behind them.

Lizard jumped into Devin's arms when she stepped out of the car and hugged her fiercely. "I have missed you so much," she cried.

Damien, Tara, and two other small children followed Lizard out of the house. "Sweet ride," he commented when he took in the car.

"A gift from Lord Jordan," Tia told him.

"Very nice," he repeated.

Win, Alix, and Marie walked over to them. "Welcome home, Marie," he said.

"Thank you, my Alpha."

Damien introduced Win and Alix to Tara and his children.

Still wrapped in Devin's arms, Lizard looked at Alix, "Are you really a black panther?"

"Yes, I really am," Alix, answered.

"That's awesome," Lizard, answered. "Can I see?"

"Later, Lizard," Damien replied. "We need to welcome our guests into our home."

"I'm sorry," Lizard said to Alix.

"No problem, I promise to show you later," Alix replied with a wink.

Marie bent down to pick up her bag. "Let me carry that for you so I can catch up with Miss Anna," Tia replied. "We have a lot to catch up on," she added.

"Yes you do," Marie said as she and Tia left the group.

"Let's take your bags and get you ladies settled in. I thought you could use the downstairs guest rooms," Damien told Devin. "You will have much more privacy that way, if you get my drift." He nodded toward Lizard.

Devin chuckled. "Do you really think being downstairs is going to keep her out of the middle of our bed?"

"You may be right," Damien laughed.

"Get settled in and I will have lunch ready in a few minutes," Tara told them.

"This place is beautiful," Alix remarked while they walked into the Alpha's home. "Thank you for having us."

"We're honored that you have joined us," Damien replied. "We hope you'll join the pack in a run tomorrow night."

"Do we have to wait until then?" she sheepishly asked Devin.

"No my friend, we will run tonight if you are up to it?"

"I need to stretch my muscles," Alix answered.

Damien led them to bedrooms on the bottom floor and they dropped their bags on the beds. "Freshen up if you like and then meet us in the kitchen for lunch."

Lizard jumped onto the bed. "I asked father if we could picnic out on the island tomorrow," she said.

"What did he say?" Devin asked.

"He told me it was up to you and your friends," she answered.

"Egg salad?"

"Nothing but," Lizard replied.

"I guess we're going on a picnic then," Devin answered.

"All right!" Lizard yelled, and fled the room.

Alix stepped into the doorway. "What did you do to her?" she asked grinning.

"We agreed you would go with us on a picnic tomorrow," Devin replied.

"Cool," Alix answered.

"Would you like to visit Doc after lunch and get your checkup out of the way?"

"Yes, that sounds like a plan," Alix answered.

"Let's eat then," Devin said and they walked into the kitchen.

†

After destroying a large stack of sandwiches, Devin took Alix and Win to meet Doc. When they stepped inside, Doc hugged them all and stood back to take a good look at Alix.

"Pardon my staring, but I haven't seen a werecat in about ten years," he said.

"No problem," Alix said. "Where did you see them?"

"I was traveling to visit another pack in Texas and I stopped at a small country store outside of Houston. A young werecat couple ran the store and I spent hours there talking with them."

"I've never seen another cat," Alix said. "I was orphaned as a child and my parents had been the last of our clan."

"Augustus is your last name. Are you any kin to Harley?" he asked.

"Harley raised me from a baby," Alix said.

"I was sorry to hear of his passing," Doc said. "He was a good man."

"Yes he was," Alix said, shifting her feet uncomfortably. Talking about her father was still difficult for her.

"Okay, ladies, if you will excuse us we will get on with Alix's checkup," Doc said, and led her into an exam room. He stopped and turned back to Win. "Don't let her play with my instruments while I'm gone please. She's been messing with them since she was a pup."

Win chuckled and nodded her head. "I'll try to keep her out of trouble."

"Thanks," Doc said and followed Alix.

"He seems to be a real character," she said to Devin.

Devin smiled. "He's been treating the pack for fifty years. Tia will be assisting him once she finishes school."

"I can only imagine the injuries he has seen over the years."

"A little bit of everything, from when I poked a lima bean up my nose to severed limbs, and he's assisted with almost every birth in the compound."

Win broke out laughing. "A lima bean, really?"

"Well it seemed like a good idea at the time," Devin said, grinning.

†

"Damien said you received blood from Devin when you were injured," Doc said when they entered the room.

"Yes, she helped save me," Alix said.

"Have you noted anything different since the transfusion?"

"Like what?" she asked.

"A desire to howl at the moon or scratch fleas?" he joked.

Alix realized he was being humorous. "No, sir, I feel just fine."

"Uh huh," he said. He took out his stethoscope and checked her vital signs, then took a little rubber hammer to check her reflexes. "Show me where you were injured."

Alix winced when she lifted the shirt over her head.

"Still a little sore?" he asked.

"Yes, sir, a bit," she answered.

Doc looked at purplish red scar lines that ran from under her navel toward her left hip. Her healing was still progressing and soon the scars would be fine white lines, no more than a scratch. His fingers gently palpated the muscles along the largest scar. Alix flinched several times and he looked up at her.

"Is it true Tia healed you?" he asked.

"Yes, the wound only healed after she laid her hand on me and she sent energy to my cat."

"This I have got to see. Have a seat and I will be right back," he told her and left the room to walk out to the waiting room.

Devin and Win jumped up when he returned without Alix. "Is she okay?" Win asked.

"Yes, she's going to be fine," he said. "Devin will you run over to Miss Anna and bring Tia back?"

"Sure," Devin said and left the office.

"What's wrong?" Win asked.

"Alix still has some pain around the scar and I think Tia can finish the healing and take away her pain," he said. "Otherwise, Alix is very healthy."

"Thank you," Win said.

"Relax and I will have her back to you in a few minutes."

He walked back down the hall to where Alix was sitting. He sat on a stool next to her. "I've sent Devin for Tia," he said. "I think she can finish the healing and take your pain away. Are you willing to let her try?"

"Sure, Doc," she said.

"Lay back then and relax until she gets here."

Alix stretched out on the exam table and closed her eyes.

Several minutes later Tia knocked on the door and came in. "What's wrong?"

"Alix still has pain and soreness around her scarring and I want you to try to finish the healing and take away her pain. Are you willing to try?"

"Yes, Doc," she said.

He stood and offered her the stool to sit next to Alix. He leaned back against the wall to watch.

"Are you ready?" she asked Alix.

"Whenever you are," Alix answered.

Tia placed her hands on Alix's skin above her scar and closed her eyes. She focused on bringing her energy to the surface and using it to take away Alix's pain. For several minutes, nothing seemed to be happening and then Tia felt her palms heating up.

Doc watched in amazement while Tia's hands began

to glow as her energy passed into Alix's body. He watched while Tia's hands caressed the full length of the damaged tissue several times and then she removed her hands and looked to Alix. "How do you feel?"

Alix lowered her hand to the scar and pressed the surrounding muscles with her fingertips. "No pain," she said, with relief in her voice.

"Sit up and raise your hands above your head," Doc instructed.

Alix sat up on the table and raised her hands above her head several times without wincing in pain. "All good," she said. "Thanks again, Tia."

"You're welcome."

"Amazing," Doc said. "I wouldn't have believed it if I hadn't seen it for myself."

Tia smiled at him.

"I think we're all done here, ladies," he said, and they walked back to the front room where Devin and Win were waiting.

"She's good as new," he announced.

"Thanks, Doc," Devin said. "Will we see you tomorrow night at the run?"

"I wouldn't miss it," he said and walked them to the door.

"I'll see you later," Tia said and kissed Devin.

They walked back to Damien's and found him and Lizard on the porch. "All good?" he asked.

"All good," Alix answered.

"Lizard and I were thinking about a boil tonight and wanted to see if you ladies would like a ride around the bayou to get some fresh crawfish?"

"We'd love it," Alix said.

"Run tell your Mom we will be back later," he said to

Lizard.

She dashed into the house and they could hear her excited voice when she told her mom where they were going. When she ran back out, she grabbed Devin's hand.

"Let's roll," Damien said, and they walked to the dock. "Grab some of those buckets please, Devin." He began untying the mooring lines. "Five should do."

Devin and Alix brought the buckets on board and, when everyone took a seat, Damien cranked the powerful motor and gunned the throttle while they raced across the bayou to some of his favorite fishing spots. The three women were a vision of beauty with the wind blowing through their dark hair. Lizard looked up at her idol, Devin, and smiled while the wind brought tears to her eyes.

"I am so glad you're home, Devin. I have missed you so," she said above the loud motor.

Devin placed a large hand on the girl's head. "I can't believe how you have grown in just a few short weeks. You'll soon be tall like me at this rate."

Lizard smiled with a look of total admiration in her eyes. Devin realized she couldn't love her more if she had given birth to her. They had always shared a special bond, one that grew with each passing year. Devin looked at her and knew that in just a few short years, she would reach puberty and Lizard would transform for the first time and finally realize what it meant to be full-blooded Were. She and Tia would be back on the compound before Lizard's rite of passage, so she could be there to witness and assist with her first transition. She looked at the child smiling up at her and thought, *damn, it seemed like just yesterday she was learning to walk.*

When Damien pulled up to the first trap, he slowed

and then cut the engine completely. "Lizard, do you and Devin care to do the honors and see what we have?"

Lizard jumped from her seat and made a dash for the front of the airboat. Devin quickly caught up to her and reached for a long branch to slow their approach. "Careful now, I don't want to have to fight the gators for you if you fall in," she teased.

"Oh Devin, you know I've done this plenty of times," Lizard said and braced her foot on the edge of the boat, just like her father had taught her. She reached out carefully for the line and struggled mightily with the weight of the trap, but Devin allowed her to bring it onboard.

"Whoa, that's a healthy batch," Devin said. "Would you mind if I helped?"

"Please," Lizard said when she realized she would not be able to empty the trap on her own.

"You grab the bucket then and I'll pour," Devin said.

The first trap nearly filled the entire first bucket, and it was a good start to their eating well in the evening.

"Don't forget we have to add bait to the trap," Devin said.

Lizard reached into a separate bucket and pulled out a smelly fish head and then dropped it in the trap.

"Be sure to rinse your hands, so you don't smell like dead fish," Devin teased as she gently lowered the trap back in place.

Lizard ran her hands through the water to rinse them and then wiped them on a towel her father held.

"Good start, you two," Damien said, and Lizard glowed with pride. "On to the next," he said after they had taken their seats.

"We are going to be eating well tonight," Alix said as she eyed the bucket. "Can I help you with the next trap?"

"Sure," Lizard said. "If it's okay with Devin."

"Be my guest, there will be plenty," Devin said with a wink.

Damien started the motor and they took a sharp turn when he headed to the next trap. Lizard took delight in pointing out large gators basking on the banks in the sunlight, and told Devin they were getting suntans.

Devin roared with laughter. "I guess they got tired of being greenish," she teased.

"I reckon so," Lizard said, and she placed her hand on Devin's knee.

Damien smiled at the obvious love they had for one another. It filled him with joy watching his baby sister and his oldest forming such a strong bond. He could not ask for a better role model for his child.

An hour later, they had their buckets filled with crawfish. "Should we pick up a few cat daddies to filet and fry too?" he asked Devin.

"I'm sure they won't go to waste," she said with a wink to Alix.

Lizard looked at Alix with a serious look on her face, and asked, "Cats love fish, don't they?"

Alix mustered every ounce of restraint she had to prevent herself from busting out in laughter, and looked back at Lizard. "Cats love fish and every other kind of meat and seafood, and lots of it," she said.

Damien smiled at his daughter. "Cat daddies here we come."

Damien located the milk jugs that marked a trotline and cut the motor on the boat while they glided smoothly through the water. Lizard jumped out of her seat, heading to the side of the boat.

"I think I'd better handle this one," Damien said and reached down to grab the jug. He pulled on the line and removed five large catfish from their captivity. They croaked at him while he carefully removed the hooks and dropped them into a live well. "You have to be careful with their spines," he told Lizard. "They can easily puncture a hand or an arm and they hurt like the dickens."

"Yes, sir," she said, and she tucked her hands in her pockets for safekeeping.

"I'll protect you," Devin cried out and swooped a giggling Lizard into her lap.

"Let's head home," Damien said, and drove like a mad man back to the dock. Lizard, Devin, Alix, and Win screamed with glee at the wild turns he took out on the water.

Tia, Marie, and Miss Anna waited for them at the docks. Devin smiled when she saw her lover and two great friends waiting for them. She stepped off the boat and helped Damien secure the mooring lines and unload the buckets containing their dinner.

"We gonna have some good eating tonight," Marie said as she watched them unload. "What can we do to help?"

Damien's Alpha persona kicked in when he started handing out orders. "You and Miss Anna can help Tara get some potatoes and corn ready for a boil. Lizard, you can make a stack of firewood by the fireplace for later." He looked at Tia and grinned. "You, my dear, can mix up a huge batch of hush puppy mix, while Devin and I skin these cats."

Alix and Win both looked up at him for their instructions. "You two," he said with a beautiful smile, "can bring us all a cold beer and keep us company while we get ready to start dinner."

"There's a large blue cooler on the deck that's probably full of beer," Devin told Alix. "Go grab a handful and Win can bring out a couple of chairs for you."

Damien grabbed another bucket and returned to the boat for the catfish while Devin pulled out a cane knife, pliers, and fileting knives.

Damien took out the first large fish and removed the head with a cane knife, dropping the head in a bucket to use for bait. He handed the first carcass to Devin who gutted the fish and then impaled the body on a large spike. She used the knife to make an incision at the base of the tail and then used the pliers to peel the tough skin down the body. She turned the fish over, repeated the process, and then laid the skinned fish on the cleaning table.

"Just like old times, Baby Sis," Damien said when he handed her the next fish.

"Yes it is," she said when she looked up at him with a grin. "I miss this time with you."

"Hopefully it won't be long before you and Tia can come home," he said, when Alix and Win returned. "Take a break, and I'll do the next one while you get a cold one in you."

Devin rinsed her hands and then reached for the cold beer Alix offered her. "Thanks," she said, sitting atop one of the deck pilings.

"It's so beautiful out here, I can see why you miss it," Alix said.

"Our families have been feasting off the bayous for generations," Devin said. "If you go hungry here, it's your own damned fault."

Alix chuckled. "You won't have to worry about that from me. I can taste those mudbugs and catfish already."

"I'm really glad you two could join us for the weekend," Damien said.

"Thanks for the invite," Win answered. "We've heard so much about the Baton Rouge Pack it's a pleasure to finally be here."

"Harley spent a good amount of time here in his younger days," he said. "I don't think even Devin was old enough to remember him, but he was a good friend to our parents."

"No, I don't remember meeting him," Devin said.

"You were still just a toddler then."

"It must have been right before he rescued me," Alix said.

"Actually, he visited right afterwards, and Miss Anna taught him how to care for you." Damien's information surprised them. "Boy, did he have his hands full with a Were toddler," he chuckled.

"So, I've been here before?" Alix said.

"Several times when you were young," he said. "You and Devin wrestled in the playpen for hours when Harley had a job to complete."

"Why am I just learning about this now?" Devin asked.

Damien shrugged. "I don't know, I guess it's taken me this long to put two and two together."

Devin looked at Alix. "I knew there had to be a reason I liked you," she teased.

"It wasn't my good looks or winning personality?" Alix asked.

"Okay, you two, it's starting to get deep in here," Win said.

"Playpen mates," Devin said and shook her head. She finished off her beer and took over for Damien. "Your turn before the beer gets warm."

Damien handed her the knife and she finished fileting

the fish, placing the large strips of boneless meat into an aluminum bowl. "Should I put these in some buttermilk to soak until it's time to cook?" she asked her brother.

"Yes, and check on the ladies to see how their activities are coming," he said. "I don't know about y'all, but I'm getting hungry."

"Okay, I'll meet you out on the deck shortly," Devin said and she carried the bowl inside.

Lizard had piled a large stack of wood by the fireplace and followed her in. The kitchen was filled with a blur of activity as Tia, Tara, Marie, and Miss Anna toiled at their tasks.

"Are we ready to start the cookers?" Devin asked while she poured buttermilk over the fish.

"We'll be ready in about five minutes," Tara said. "Tell my handsome husband to light the fires."

"I'm sure he'll be pleased to do that," Devin said with a wink.

"You know him well," Tara said and smiled.

"Off we go, Lizard," Devin yelled and raced her niece to the deck. "Tara said light her fire or something like that," she told a grinning Damien.

"Got it under control," Damien said, and lit the propane beneath two large cookers.

Devin and Damien cooked for the group, preparing fried hush puppies and catfish to accompany a boil of the crawfish, potatoes, and corn. Tia and Lizard spread butcher paper across several tables while Tara and Win brought out plates, condiments, and tea for those who wanted something other than beer.

When they sat down to feast, Damien reached for Tara's hand on his right and Lizard's hand on his left, and the remainder of the group joined hands. "Our heavenly spirit guides, we thank you for this bounty from your womb, and the company of good friends while we feast tonight in your honor. Protect us and keep our hearts strong."

Darkness fell while they were feasting and an hour after they had eaten, the moon rose.

Alix looked at Devin. "Are you up for a run?" she asked.

"Always," Devin answered and looked at Damien. "Would you care to join us?"

"Tomorrow night. I have a fire to light tonight," he said with a devious grin.

Lizard looked at Devin with longing. "Soon you'll be able to run with us, little one, but tonight you will have to ride. Is it okay if she joins us?" she asked Damien.

"Just try leaving without her," Damien teased. "Yes, but don't wear Devin out, Lizard."

"We'll be back later," Devin told Tia and kissed her softly.

"Are you sure you are healed enough?" Win asked.

"After today, I'm fine, thanks to Tia."

Win smiled at her lover. "Be safe then, and hurry back to me."

"I will," Alix grinned when she leaned down to kiss Win.

†

Alix and Devin undressed and left their clothing on the hood of the SUV. "Don't forget to hold on tight," Devin told Lizard just before she shifted into her wolf.

Lizard watched while Alix shifted and a gasp left her

body. "You are beautiful," she stated while her hands stroked the cat's soft coat.

Devin let out a chuffing sound and sat down to allow Lizard to climb onto her back and wrap her arms around her neck. She stood and shook to make sure the child was secure and then took off at a trot. When they left the buildings of the compound behind, Devin picked up speed until they were loping down a familiar trail. The moon glowed above them while the pair ran shoulder to shoulder with an exceptionally happy young girl clinging to Devin's neck.

When they approached the fork in the path that lead to the Devil's Tree, Alix skidded to a halt and shifted. "What is it that I sense down that path?"

Devin sat on her back haunches while Lizard slid off her back. "That would be the Devil's Tree," Lizard replied while Devin shifted back to human form.

"Go on," she urged Lizard.

"It's a tree that has been on our boundary for hundreds of years. It can't be destroyed and people come to the tree to do evil," Lizard told her, with a voice just higher than a whisper.

"That was actually pretty good," Devin praised her young niece.

"People who wish to enter a pact with the devil come to this tree to ask for special powers or gifts. When the bargain is struck, the person places their hand on the rough bark of the tree and their bloodied handprint glows red against the bark to seal the deal with the devil."

Alix listened with interest to both Lizard's and Devin's story.

"It's also where my grandparents were killed, and Dad and Devin took revenge on the witch that killed them."

"Is it a problem for us to go there?" Alix asked.

Devin looked at Lizard. "Are you okay with it?"

Lizard nodded. "I'm safe with you."

"Yes you are." She looked at Alix. "It's not far so let's walk."

Lizard walked between them and took each of their hands in hers while they walked down the path. Devin's hackles rose like they always did when she entered the clearing. Devin's eyes drew to the spot where her parents had died, which remained bare, marking the place where they fell.

"That is where they died," Lizard told Alix.

"A part of them remains here, doesn't it?" Alix asked.

"Yes, to warn us of danger," Devin answered. Her eyes drifted to the tree, thankful that there was no sign of a bloodied handprint.

Alix looked at the tree. The gnarled limbs and blackened bark reeked of evil. She remembered Harley speaking of it when she was a child, but she had always thought it was a story to scare her. "Harley told me about this, but I never realized it was real."

"It is very much real," Devin assured her.

"Thank you for showing me," Alix replied. She realized how uncomfortable Devin was and turned to her. "Let's run," she cried out and shifted back to her cat.

Devin shifted and, with a final look at the tree and Lizard on her back, she fled the sad memories of the clearing. She raced to catch up with Alix.

While they ran, Alix worried about the weight of Lizard on Devin's back.

'*No need to worry,*' Devin projected without thinking.

Alix slid to a halt and stared at Devin. '*We can do this?*'

'*We are doing it so I guess so,*' Devin answered.

'*This is freaking awesome,*' Alix replied.

'*We must be more closely bonded since we have exchanged blood,*' Devin supposed.

'*Do we tell the others or keep it a secret for now?*'

'*Let's keep it between us for now,*' Devin answered.

"Are you two okay?" Lizard asked when they stood there staring at each other.

Devin nodded to answer Lizard and they trotted down the path. She and Alix chatted light-heartedly while they ran, still amazed at their new abilities.

They ran for another hour circling the boundary of the compound and returned to Damien's house. After shifting, they dressed and walked into the house, Lizard walking between them.

Devin projected a thought to Alix and when she did not respond, she learned the limits of their projections. They could only communicate silently when they shifted and not in human form.

"Interesting," she commented to Alix. "Only when we are shifted."

"I'll still take it," Alix stated with a grin while they walked onto the porch.

"Looks like we're the last ones up," Devin said when they entered the quiet house. "I'm going to tuck Lizard in and I will see you in the morning."

Alix walked into the bedroom she and Win were sharing.

Devin took Lizard's hand when they climbed the stairs. "Thank you for taking me tonight," Lizard said when they reached her room. "I can't wait to change so I can run with you as wolf."

"Soon, little one, soon," Devin promised. "Go brush your teeth and get your pajamas on and I will tuck you into bed."

She sat on the edge of the bed until Lizard emerged from the bathroom and climbed onto the bed and between the sheets. "Get some rest. Tomorrow is going to be a long day."

"Thanks for coming home, Devin," Lizard replied and then she pulled her down and kissed her cheek.

"I will always come home," Devin promised her, and tucked the sheets around her tightly. "Goodnight, Lizard."

"Goodnight, Devin, I love you," she answered.

"I love you too."

Damien lay back against the headboard of his bed and smiled when he heard the exchange between Lizard and Devin. *'Goodnight, Baby Sis,'* he projected to Devin.

'Goodnight, my Alpha, I love you.'

'Love you too.'

When she entered the downstairs bedroom, Tia was sleeping soundly. She slipped out of her clothes, and curled her body around Tia and breathed in her scent. "Mine," she whispered.

"Yours," Tia answered and pulled Devin's arm around her waist.

Chapter Sixteen

Saturday blossomed into another beautiful day. They all packed a picnic lunch of egg salad sandwiches, chips, and tea, and then rode in airboats to the island that Damien and Devin had dubbed Treasure Island when they were children.

Lizard, Alix, and Devin explored the island while the rest of the group relaxed on the small strip of sandy beach. When the afternoon began to fade, they returned to the compound and started to prepare for a cookout. Damien had planned to grill steaks before the pack assembled for their weekly group run.

Tia and Win assisted in the kitchen while Alix, Lizard, and Devin kept Damien company on the deck. "This place is so peaceful," Alix commented when she stretched out on a lounger. "Makes me homesick for the farm."

"You will be there soon, my friend," Devin reminded her.

"Don't forget, you and Tia promised to visit."

"We'll come up the first break she gets from school," Devin replied.

"I'll look forward to that."

Damien joined them while they waited for the coals to burn down. "Will you and Win take a break from hunting for a while?"

"I hope at least for a month or so," Alix replied. "You never know in this business though."

"I understand and I hope you both know you are welcome to stop in at any time when you are in the area."

"We'll definitely be dropping in from time to time," she assured him.

Lizard crawled into Devin's lap and looked at her father. "Will there be a bonfire tonight?"

"Yes, I hear the men preparing for it already," Damien answered. He turned back to Alix. "The children and those not wishing to run tell stories around the fire while the pack runs."

"Win will enjoy that," Alix replied with the warm smile she had when she spoke of her lover.

†

Later, after they had finished a delicious steak dinner, the pack assembled at the fire until full darkness was upon them. The pack shifted then, and with their Alpha leading the way, they ran, one shimmering mass of fur and muscle under the light of a brilliant moon.

The children were asleep, tucked in their beds, when Damien and the pack returned to the bonfire. Damien lifted his muzzle to the stars and howled, followed one by one by each of the pack.

Tia smiled at the beautiful sound and knew her love would be coming to her soon.

†

Sunday morning dawned with the sound of heavy machinery. Pack members were using a backhoe to dig pits to roast the large hogs freshly butchered for the celebration. They would cook slowly all day while the pack put together dishes and desserts to accompany the meat.

The compound buzzed with activity while tables were set up in the courtyard and another large bonfire was prepared. Tia had disappeared earlier with Marie and Miss Anna, and Devin wandered around the compound helping where she could. Devin was setting up a table, when Alix and Win arrived and she took them around the compound to introduce them to pack members.

"Don't worry, there won't be a test later," Devin teased them.

They were carrying wood to the roasting pit when Devin heard the rumble of a motorcycle and looked up to see Lucia and Kaitlin riding down the drive. Lucia pulled up behind Tia's new car and parked the bike. She quickly dismounted and offered Kaitlin her hand.

"You two made excellent time," Devin grinned.

"We didn't want to miss out on anything," Lucia teased.

Kaitlin looked around at all the activity going on around them. "This place is amazing," she uttered in awe.

"Come, let us show you around, and introduce you," Devin said.

Lizard flew out of the house and Kaitlin watched her run to Devin. "Let me guess, this is Lizard."

"The one and only," Devin replied. "These are my

friends, Kaitlin and Lucia," Devin told her niece.

"You are wolf," she said to Lucia, "but you aren't." Lizard cocked her head to look at Kaitlin.

"Just a plain old human," Kaitlin replied with a warm smile.

"Don't believe her, there's nothing plain about her," Devin chuckled while she hugged her friend.

"What is that fantastic smell?" Lucia asked.

"Four whole hogs that are roasting today for tonight's feast," Devin answered.

"What are you going to eat?" Lucia teased her.

"I think there will be plenty for everyone," Devin answered.

Lucia looked around at all the activity. "Is there anything we can do to help?"

"I think our best bet is to try to stay out of everyone's way. The pack is on the move and they will call for us if they need help." Devin walked with them to chairs under a large shade tree. "Can I get you something to drink?"

"I could use some water," Kaitlin replied.

Devin looked at Lucia. "You ready for a beer?"

"No, I think I'll stick with water too for now."

Devin looked at Lizard. "Will you bring us four bottles of water?"

"Sure, Devin," she answered and flew across the yard.

Kaitlin watched her and smiled. "She looks just like you."

"More every day," Damien answered, when he walked up behind them. "I think I should be worried."

"I don't know, I think Devin turned out okay," Kaitlin replied.

Damien smiled at his sister. "That she did. I could not

be more proud of her. I'm glad that you were able to join us today," he told Kaitlin and Lucia.

"We are honored for the invitation," Lucia answered.

"There will be some live music in a few minutes, so sit back and relax and let us know if there is anything that we can get you."

Lizard came rushing back with an armful of bottled water.

"There you are, my little one," Damien said to her. "I was hoping that you would honor me with a dance, unless Jacob has already asked for your first dance."

Lizard blushed profusely.

"Who is Jacob?" Devin asked.

"Thomas's son. He's a year older than Lizard and has taken quite a shine to her."

Lizard passed out the water. "He hasn't asked yet," she told her father.

"Good, so you are all mine." He lifted her into his strong arms. "Are you too old to dance with your father?"

"Never," Lizard grinned and she kissed his cheek.

He placed her back on the ground. "I will find you when the music starts up." He looked at Devin. "Where's Tia?"

She laughed. "Probably holed up with Marie and Miss Anna somewhere. There's no telling what they're up to."

"I think you should go find them and remind them this is a celebration that they need to participate in. They can do all their hocus pocus stuff later."

"Yes, my Alpha," Devin answered and stood from her chair. "I will be right back, ladies."

"Do you think they're practicing magic?" Lizard ran

along beside Devin while she walked across the compound in search of Tia and her teachers.

"I don't know, but we're about to find out," Devin said when they arrived at Miss Anna's home.

"Come in," Anna said when Devin raised her hand to knock.

She and Lizard walked in to find all three women sitting around the kitchen table drinking coffee. "The Alpha has sent me to remind you of the celebration going on outside," she told them.

"We were just discussing making our grand entrance," Marie answered with a chuckle.

"The music is about to start and then the eating will follow. I think there will be a surprise after nightfall," Devin hinted.

"What surprise?" Lizard asked.

"If I told you, it wouldn't be a surprise, now would it?"

"No Devin," she answered, disappointed.

"You won't be disappointed, I promise," she told her niece. "Ladies, it's time for us to move to the courtyard and join the pack."

They stood from around the table and joined Lizard and Devin walking back to the courtyard. Hundreds of people were moving around and a small band was warming up on the stage.

"Do you like Jacob?" Devin asked Lizard.

"He's all right for a boy," she answered, but her cheeks flushed again.

"You'll have to point him out to me. I'm not sure I remember him," Devin stated.

Lizard looked up at her. "He's the shirtless one over by the bonfire pile," she answered.

Devin looked over at the young boy. "He's handsome."

"Yeah, he is," Lizard replied with a dreamy quality to her voice.

Tia slipped her hand into Devin's and smiled at her lover. "Does someone have her first crush?" she asked Devin.

"Maybe," she smiled.

The music started to play and Lizard scanned the crowd for her father. When she saw him standing over by the cooking pit, she ran up to him.

Damien saw her approach and he bent down to talk to her. "Are we ready to dance?"

"Yes, Father." She smiled.

Damien lifted her into his arms when they reached the dance area and he moved gracefully with her in his arms to the beat of the soft music. Damien looked into her eyes.

"You are growing up too fast, my dear. Soon I won't be able to get a dance from you without having to beat the boys away."

"I will always dance with you, Father," she answered sweetly. "You will always be my first love."

Damien held her close, fighting back the tears until the dance was over. He placed her gently on the ground and whispered, "Jacob is coming your way. I love you, Lizard."

"I love you too, Dad," she replied and turned when Jacob walked next to her.

"Good evening, my Alpha," he spoke to Damien and then turned to Lizard. "Will you dance with me?" he asked.

"Sure," Lizard said and took his hand while they danced awkwardly to the music.

Devin walked over and hugged Damien. "When did

she grow up so much?"

"I don't know, I thought I was watching her closely."

"You have to admit, they make a cute couple."

"Jacob would make a good match for Lizard, but I'm in no hurry for her to fall in love," he commented.

"It may be too late for that." Devin sighed while she watched the young pair dance. "Did the fireworks arrive as planned?"

"Yeah, they did. Thomas and Drew have them all set up for later."

"The kids are going to love that."

"Yes they will." Damien looked through the crowd. "Have you seen Tara?"

Devin nodded toward the food tables. "Guarding the desserts," she teased.

✝

The afternoon faded into early evening and when it was time to announce the beginning of the feast, Damien stepped on stage. The entire audience hushed when they saw him take the microphone in hand.

"Greetings, my pack," he said, his strong voice reverberating through the crowd. "Tonight we welcome home some of our pack, and new friends of the pack. Most of you know that Devin has been in New Orleans for some time now, and she and her friends have brought great honor to our pack."

Many heads in the crowd turned to look and smile at Devin and her friends.

"I would ask that Marie, Devin, Tia, Alix, Win, Lucia, and Kaitlin please stand."

The women stood as requested.

"These are our heroes and this is their story. The Vampire Clan and the Baton Rouge Pack have recently been in danger from a powerful vampire, a traitor from Lord Jordan's clan, and three rogue Weres who desired to take over not only New Orleans, but our pack as well."

Growls rose throughout the crowd at this news.

"Lord Jordan, head of the clan in New Orleans, hired Alix, our werecat sister, and Win, the mighty hunter from Monroe, to deal with this threat, but when they realized the identity of the vampire that threatened our futures, they sought the assistance of Tia, our spell binder, and Devin."

The crowd chuffed and nodded their approval.

"Our sister, Marie, who has been away from us for far too long, was able to assist Tia in learning a spell that would greatly enhance the group's chance of victory, and together they defeated the enemy, but not without a cost. Alix was injured in the battle and Lucia, from the Houma pack, and Tia were successful in healing her wounds and saving her life." He smiled at Kaitlin. "While not directly involved in the battle, our friend Kaitlin provided great friendship and support to Tia, Devin, and Lucia."

Kaitlin blushed from being included in the story.

"Tonight, my pack, we celebrate their victory, their courage, and their commitment to the strength of our pack. Welcome home, friends and family. Tonight we feast in your honor."

The crowd erupted with applause and whistles, until Damien raised his hand. "Dear Heavenly Spirits above, and those that have passed before us, please bless this food we are about to eat and protect our pack and friends. Now ladies and gentlemen, let's eat."

People flocked to the tables to begin filling plates, while others came over to Devin and company to offer their appreciation and congratulations on their victory. All of the children and several of the adults had commented that they had never seen a werecat before, so Alix excused herself and walked into the privacy of their room and shifted. When she returned to the group, she sat between Win and Lizard, who stood next to Devin. Lizard stroked down her back with her small hand.

"Isn't she beautiful?" she said when her young friends came for a closure look.

The sun was setting when the bonfire roared to life, and the pack settled in for a hearty meal. The band played throughout the meal. When every appetite was sated and the pack settled into their seats, Damien again took the stage.

"Tonight we have a very special treat for young and old alike," he said.

A loud pop sounded from somewhere behind the stage and the first of many fireworks streaked through the air. For thirty minutes, the skies above the compound filled with the colorful display, with many sounds of delight coming from the pack.

Lizard had climbed up in Devin's lap and her eyes lit with excitement while she watched the fireworks and enjoyed the closeness of her idol. When the fireworks display ended, the young returned home for the evening, and the adults enjoyed a few additional hours of merriment.

It was well after midnight before Devin and her friends decided to call it a night and get some rest. Lucia and Kaitlin were placed in rooms in the Alpha house, and they all settled in for a restful night.

†

The following morning, Devin awoke to the smell of cooking bacon, and she left the bedroom to find Damien and Tara in the kitchen preparing breakfast for everyone. Tara was cooking bacon while Damien cooked pancakes.

"Good morning." He smiled when she entered the kitchen. "Grab a cup of coffee and join us."

"It smells delicious," she replied when she walked to the coffee pot. "Thank you again for last night. That was a fantastic celebration."

"Yes, it was," Damien, agreed with a grin. "We should do that more often."

"May I help with anything?"

"You can start waking the others. Breakfast is just about ready."

Devin left the kitchen and moved from room to room, waking her friends and inviting them to breakfast. When she reached the room she and Tia shared, she sat on the edge of the bed.

"My love," she whispered, "it's time to get up for breakfast."

Tia rolled over and opened her eyes. "Good morning." She stretched lazily. "Is it really already time to leave?"

"Not until Damien has filled our bellies one more time," Devin teased.

Tia stretched again and smiled at Devin. "One day we will never have to leave."

"Yes, one day soon." Devin smiled with pride at her lover. "I do believe you are looking forward to that as much as I am."

"This is home," Tia stated.

"Yes it is," she answered. "I need to go get Lizard up, and we will meet you in the kitchen."

"I'll be right there," Tia replied and kissed Devin.

Devin left the bedroom to go upstairs to wake Lizard. She knocked softly and entered the room to find her niece crying on the bed.

"What's the matter?" Devin asked.

"I don't want you to go today," she pouted.

Devin took Lizard in her arms. "I will be coming back whenever I can," she promised.

"I know, but I miss you so much." She spoke between sniffles.

"I miss you too, but you are strong and have been doing a great job with your little brother and sister. Your mom needs your help."

"I know," she repeated.

"I guess if you can't make it down to breakfast, I'll have to eat your share of pancakes."

"Father's making pancakes?"

"They will be ready by the time we get there," Devin answered.

Lizard climbed off her lap, put her feet in her slippers, and reached for Devin's hand. "Let's go," she said with a smile.

✝

After breakfast, everyone started packing for home. Win and Alix were excited about going back to the farm and were the first to leave. Tia and Devin walked out with them after they had made their goodbyes to Damien and his family.

"I know you're excited to get back home, but you are welcome here or in New Orleans any time you care to visit," Devin reminded them.

"Thank you, my friend," Alix replied and hugged her close. "I look forward to you two visiting us soon."

"We will be there," Tia promised.

"Thank you for everything." Win hugged them both. "Especially what you did for Alix. I would have been lost without her."

Releasing Win from the embrace, Devin looked into her eyes. "Just let me know if she starts howling at the moon."

Win chuckled. "I will."

"Be safe and give us a call soon," Devin told them when they reached the SUV.

"We will," Alix replied as she held the door for Win.

"Drive safe," Tia called out.

Devin wrapped her arm around Tia's waist while they watched their friends drive away. "I miss them already."

"I do too," Tia agreed. She took Devin's hand and they walked toward the house. "Are you ready to begin the separation process with Lizard?"

"No, not really, it rips my heart apart to see her cry."

"I'll take the car and go collect Marie if you want to bring our bags out. Kaitlin can ride with us unless she wants to ride back with Lucia."

"I'll check with them and we'll be ready when you return."

Devin walked back into the house. "Do you want to ride with us, Kaitlin?"

"Nope, I'm going to ride with the one that brought

me," she laughed.

"Okay, Tia will be back in just a few minutes."

Lizard ran up to her and climbed into her arms. "I'll hate it when you get too big to hug me like this," Devin said.

"I will never be that big."

"Remember what we talked about this morning."

"I will," she answered with tears welling in her eyes.

"You are a strong young wolf. Never forget that."

"I won't," she replied and walked over to her mother.

Damien took Devin in her arms. "The days went by too fast."

"We will be back soon," she promised. "Thanks again for a great celebration."

"We are very proud of you all," he told her.

They heard Tia pull up in the drive and started to carry the bags outside. When Devin stepped off the porch, she was surprised to look up to find the courtyard filled with her pack. As one, they lifted their faces to the morning sun and howled. Their beautiful music filled the air and gave Devin chill bumps.

Devin and Lucia answered their calls and Devin looked at Damien with tears in her eyes. "That was special," she told him.

"They are your pack and they love you," he reminded her.

"Mine," she agreed and hugged him one last time.

The End

About the Author

Ali Spooner

Ali Spooner, a native of Florida, is currently living and working in Memphis, TN. As an "Indie" author, Ali has been writing for many years as a hobby, and with the assistance of the Affinity team she has taken her love of storytelling to a new level.

Ali's characters range from cowgirls and psychics to a healthy dose of supernatural beings. She has written both stand-alone titles and series. Ali is an avid reader and her other hobbies include photography, outdoor activities, and watching college sports.

Other Books from Affinity eBook Press

Keeping Faith by TJ Vertigo
Join the antics of Reece, Faith, Cori, Vi, and even The Animal, one last time in *Keeping Faith*. Faith has finally made the big screen, but how will Reece handle her success? Will the love that they share be enough to save their relationship and soothe The Animal?

The Circle Dance by Jen Silver
Jamie Steele has moved to another town, trying to forget the heartbreak of losing her lover of six years. Sasha Fairfield finds her thoughts taken up with her ex-lover and thinks she wants Jamie back. Follow this captivating romance as love dances through the lives of these women to its surprising conclusion.

Search for the White Moon by Natalie London
Kathryn Austin, a government agent, is given opera singer, Adriana Desi, as her new assignment. Their lives and futures are in danger as the White Moon terrorists hunt them. Immerse yourself in this fast-paced romantic thriller by debut author Natalie London.

Take Me As I Am by JM Dragon & Erin O'Reilly

When Jo Lackerly and Thea Danvers meet, an unexpected friendship develops, proving a catalyst for both women to change their lives irrevocably. Follow them on a journey of discovery that will have your heart smiling, blood boiling, and senses entangled in a wonderful romance.

Carved in Stone by Jen Silver
Join the characters from *Starting Over* and *Arc Over Time* in this final book from the Starling Hill trilogy. Ellie Winters thinks she might be going mad when the ancient queen wants a proper burial for herself and her consort. *Carved in Stone* has romance, adventure, a treasure hunt, and a happy endings for all, living and dead.

Anywhere, Everywhere by Renee MacKenzie
Gwen Martin's life in the Ten Thousand Islands area changes irrevocably when Piper Jackson comes into her life. Without trust, can the budding relationship between Gwen and Piper survive? Or will the answers to the questions continue to haunt them?

Venus Rising by Ali Spooner
Levi Johnson arrives at Venus Rising, an exclusive lesbian-only tropical resort in the Virgin Islands and finds more than she expected—a sizzling hot love triangle. Torn between her attraction to two women, she struggles to choose the right woman to share her life.

The Devil's Tree by Ali Spooner
Torn between her love for the pack and her need to find what's missing in her life, Devin Benoit travels to New

Orleans. Will the previous happenings at the Devil's Tree help or hinder Devin in the fight of her life, and the life of Tia, the woman who now owns her heart?

The Beggars' Coppice by Erica Lawson
Edda Case is a woman in crisis who discovers that things are not as they seem. Is it truly a message for her from beyond the grave or is something more sinister taking place? Can Edda solve the mystery of *The Beggars' Coppice*?

Locked Inside by Annette Mori
How much does the power of love matter to someone who must overcome obstacles far greater than most people face in a lifetime.

Line of Sight by Ali Spooner
Sasha and her lover Kara are back. Continue the thrilling adventures of this couple from the Sasha Thibodaux series.

Requiem for Vukovar by Angela Koenig
Requiem for Vukovar continues the Refraction series and the exploits of Jeri O'Donnell and her partner, Kelly Corcoran. In an epic siege largely ignored by the wider world, Kelly, who was prepared to give up comforts and certainties when she became part of Jeri's nomadic life, encounters more than physical danger. Her ability to maintain her core integrity is assaulted by the inevitable ugliness of war. For Jeri, the true battle is confronting her attraction to violence as she struggles against losing herself in the exhilaration of combat.

Against All Odds by JM Dragon
From award-winning and bestselling author JM Dragon, with significant updates by Erin O'Reilly, comes an original tale of romance where everything seems to be stacked against two women whose destinies bring them together. Life however takes a twisted path, setting both Steph and Louise in directions they never thought possible. Will love win out against all odds or will love be forever lost?

The Settlement by Ali Spooner
The outpouring of love and friendship toward Cadin helps her on her path to healing and learning to trust her heart to love once again. Join bestselling author Ali Spooner on this sensational journey that ends with a heartwarming romance.

Once Upon a Time by Alane Hotchkin
Raven only wanted to escape the blows that life had dealt her. She longed to be on the open sea and free. When she came upon a beautiful young girl sitting alone in the middle of a meadow, little did she know that her destiny would be changed forever. Will they become the pawns of the ancient vision or will both paths lead to the same port of destiny? Find out in this exciting high seas adventure that will capture your imagination.

Asset Management by Annette Mori
Follow the twists and turns to the explosive conclusion. Not everything is black and white. There are many shades of gray, and sometimes it's difficult to decipher who is good and who is evil. No one is all virtue or all malevolence, but sometimes love helps us rise above.

Do Dreams Come True? by JM Dragon
How do two people who really shouldn't get on end up in a relationship? Find out in this deliciously ordinary romance.

Return to Me by Erin O'Reilly
Will Salvation bring just that to Ellie, allowing her to find peace and happiness again, or will it have her questioning all that she believes in? A wonderful romance cloaked within an intriguing mystery.

Arc Over Time by Jen Silver
Book 2 of the Starling Hill Trilogy. This wonderful romantic continuation with the characters from *Starting Over* ties up loose ends. But the question is—does everyone have a happy ending? A must read.

The Presence by Charlene Neal
Can Rebecca and Kayleigh overcome ghosts from the past and their own insecurities, or will a presence from the past tear them apart?

A Walk Away by Lacey Schmidt
Sometimes chance brings you to the right person to help you resolve some of your baggage, and you learn to like yourself a little more. Kat and Rand are smart enough to recognize this chance in each other, but they also find that there is a catch to every opportunity—walking toward something is always walking away from something else.

Possessing Morgan by Erica Lawson
The investigation has barely begun when Andrea becomes the target of a nearly fatal hit-and-run. But was it really aimed at her? Can she and Morgan find the common ground they need to solve the case and stop the attacks, or are the gaps just too wide to bridge?

Twenty-three Miles by Renee MacKenzie
This is a story about community, and how it comes together in dangerous and devastating times. When you don't know who to trust, you better have friends who will rally around you. Will Talia and Shay find the answers they need to the mystery of the murders on the parkway, or will justice be elusive? Will they survive their quest for the truth?

Reece's Star by TJ Vertigo
Under Faith's guiding, loving hand, will Reece successfully traverse the rocky road of emotion and embrace the positive changes in her life? Or will she panic and be unable to control that Animal part of herself? Will she take that next step to declare herself fully capable of love and devotion? This third installment in the popular series that began with *Private Dancer* continues the passionate and often hilarious romance of Reece and Faith as they both grow in love and in trust.

Confined Spaces by Renee MacKenzie
Corporate politics, complicated romance, and long distances conspire to keep Andie and Kara all boxed in. Can love triumph despite the Confined Spaces?

Cowgirl Up by Ali Spooner
Ride along with the MC2, for boot scootin', butt kickin', dirt eatin', rodeo adventures, with a love story thrown into the mix.

If I Were a Boy by Erin O'Reilly
Will Katie and Helen be able to make a life together work or succumb to doubts and the pressures of family? This story will fill you with the thrill of passion and the tenderness of love.

The Chronicles of Ratha: Book 2 A Lion Among the Lambs by Erica Lawson
Can Jordana believe in herself like her Noorthi sisters do? Only then can she fulfill her destiny as The Chosen One. Follow the colorful cast of characters in this action-packed adventure sequel as they traverse the galaxy. Of course, nothing ever goes smoothly when Jordana is involved.

Terminal Event by Ali Spooner
Will the killer be caught or continue to evade authorities? Can Tally and Blair's budding romance survive the possibility? Read this intense murder mystery romance and find out.

Love Forever, Live Forever by Annette Mori
Fate intervenes and puts Nicky directly back into the path of her first love, Sara, and the corresponding events send her into a tailspin. Now she must decide—who will be the person she ends up living with and loving forever?

The One by JM Dragon
2015 GCLS Winner for Romance, Intrigue, and Adventure.
The One is a romance with everything, love, intrigue, misunderstandings with a happy conclusion—the only question—who gets the girl?

Reflected Passion by Erica Lawson
Through a mirror, Françoise embraces life anew, while for Dale it is a powerful awakening, forcing her to discover not only her sensual nature, but the inner strength she possesses.

Flight by Renee Mackenzie
Some lives will be lost and others changed forever when the sisters' lives intersect. Will they be consumed by the wreckage, or will they be able to pick themselves up and take flight?

Starting Over by Jen Silver
Book 1 of the Starling Hill Trilogy. There's a mystery afoot—whose royal resting place is disturbed at Starling Hill? All is revealed in this classic romance of simmering passions, anguished loss, and the wonder of love.

E-Books, Print, Free e-books

Visit our website for more publications available online.

www.affinityebooks.com

Published by Affinity E-Book Press NZ LTD
Canterbury, New Zealand

Registered Company 2517228

www.ingramcontent.com/pod-product-compliance
Lightning Source LLC
Chambersburg PA
CBHW051539260626
47170CB00003B/1018